CHI-TOWN COYOTE

by

Heather Augustyn

Chapter 1: The Hole in the Woods

"Sebastian, over here!" The young coyotes were huddled around a small hole in the ground.

"Where?" said Sebastian, as he ran over to the hole where the rest of his friends stood.

"Right here, beside this tree root, down this hole," said Roman, who was Sebastian's closest friend and who was never afraid to look for new adventures and discoveries.

"Really, Sebastian, I think I saw it go down this hole too—he's not fooling you," said Dominic, Sebastian's older brother and the leader of the group. Sebastian stood cautiously over the hole. He knew he shouldn't be so scared, but he just couldn't help it. He kept imagining the dark hole and the chipmunk that waited inside, ready to dart out and bite him in the nose—again! Sebastian was frustrated at himself. He was scared of a little chipmunk in front of all of his friends, and his big brother.

"Why should I be so scared of a little chipmunk," he thought. After all, Sebastian was a big coyote, strong, and quick. He was taller and heavier than most coyotes—even bigger than Dominic, who was a whole year older than Sebastian.

Sebastian had thick grey-brown fur over his head and back and his tail was jet black in the summertime, but lighter now that it was winter, so he could better blend in with his surroundings. His eyes were piercing yellow, flashing and slanty with deep black, big pupils that saw everything—even the chipmunk.

Sebastian had seen the little creature dart down the hole in the earth, but he pretended he hadn't. He was afraid. Only one month earlier, Sebastian had been playing with Dominic and Roman and Tobias and Reginald, his other two friends, and he got bit on the nose. Sebastian chased the chipmunk into the hole—he had sprinted across the prairie so fast that he thought he could grab the chipmunk before it disappeared, but Sebastian was a second too slow and the chipmunk descended below the earth.

So Sebastian stuck his pointy, tapered, black snout into the opening of the hole to sniff out the chipmunk and "Bam!" the chipmunk fiercely sunk his tiny, jagged teeth into the soft, wet flesh of Sebastian's nose. At first he wasn't sure what happened because it felt so strange. But then when he saw the droplets of blood on the yellow leaves on the ground, and when he heard his friends gasp and howl, he knew he had been bit. A big coyote had been attacked by a piddly ball of fur!

Now, here Sebastian stood again over a chipmunk hole. "Sorry guys, I, uh, gotta run. I just remembered I have something way more important to do. I can't play around with a dumb hole in the ground." Sebastian took off, sprinting as fast as he could into the woods before Dominic and the guys could say anything. Or worse—laugh.

Chapter 2: Afraid

"Sebastian, where have you been? I've been so worried about you. Your brother has been home for an hour already and he said you were out doing something important—is everything okay?" Sebastian's mother was very upset since it was long past dusk and Sebastian's dinner was cold and uneaten. "We all had to eat without you, Sebastian, and you know how I feel about that— you know how important it is for us to all eat together as a family and talk about how our day went," said Sebastian's mother.

"I know, mom, I'm sorry. I didn't mean to. I just had a lot on my mind and needed some time alone to think," said Sebastian.

"That sounds serious, Sebastian—is it anything you want to talk about?" said his mother.

"No, mom, I'm okay. I just came to the conclusion that I need to be brave, like Dominic. I'm not a baby coyote anymore. I'm a big coyote," said Sebastian.

"Yes, you are," said his mother, "and I want you to know I'm very proud of you. And I'm very happy you're home—I've missed you! Now go around the back off the den. Your father wondered where you were too."

Sebastian walked to the back of his family den, a warm hut of mud and sticks positioned in a crevasse along the side of a ravine that was passed down to his family by Mr. Peri, the badger who moved down stream to be closer to his sister. Sebastian didn't want to tell his dad that he ran away from a chipmunk. He knew he should be strong and make his dad proud, and now he was afraid his dad would think he was a baby coyote. But then again, he had been bitten, so it was natural to be afraid.

"Hi dad," said Sebastian.

His dad stood tall on his thick paws, his bushy grey tail sloping downward, as it did on all coyotes. Sebastian sat down on the maple leaves that kept their den floor warm and glanced down at his own paws, then at the leaves, then up at his dad—he was nervous about what his dad might say.

"Sebastian," said his dad, "I'm happy to see you." His dad was digging into the ground at the back of the den, trying to extend their home for a bit more living space. But he had stopped now and was facing Sebastian. "Where have you been, pup—I've been worried about you?" Sebastian knew he had to tell.

"Dad, I just decided to take a walk through the woods by myself. I had to think about some things. I was with Dominic and Roman and the guys and, well, I got a little scared over a measly chipmunk again. I just keep remembering that bite—and the guys wanted time to get it and dig up its hole and I just couldn't do it, so I took off and spent some time by myself. But I want you to know I'm not a baby coyote—and I'm going to try to be brave and courageous like Dominic and stop being such a chicken. I want you to be proud of me, dad." Sebastian just let it all out. And he felt better. He wasn't sure what his dad would say, but he felt pretty good about getting it off of his big, furry chest.

"Sebastian," his dad spoke, "you know that I am always proud of you. I always have been. I understand how a chipmunk could be scary, especially after getting bit by one. I never told anyone this before, but I'll tell you." Sebastian's ears perked up even higher and were pointier than before.

"Yeah, dad?" he said eagerly.
"Well, I'm afraid of bees."
"Bees? Why, dad, they're so small!"
His dad spoke in a calm voice, "Well Sebastian, when I was a pup and I was playing with your Uncle Claudius and your Uncle Sal, I found a bees' nest, full of honey. I thought I could eat the honey and no one would notice. But a swarm of maybe 30 bees came out of that nest and the first bee stung me, right on my black nose. And I howled! I took off so fast for the river and jumped right in and hung out until it was safe. Ever since then, even to this very day, I've been afraid of bees."

"Dad, I had no idea," said Sebastian. "I thought you weren't scared of anything."

"Everybody is scared of something, Sebastian, but you can still be brave and strong and adventurous. Just be yourself, Sebastian. What makes you scared and what makes you strong, well that's just who you are and we love that."

"Thanks, dad," said Sebastian. "I know you're proud of me and I'll always make you proud."

"I know you will, pup—now what do you say we practice that howling?" said Sebastian's father.

"Alright!" said Sebastian.

"Try it like this, pup—whoo, whoo, whooodooo!" yodeled Sebastian's father.

Sebastian tried to mimic, "Whoop, whoop, woo hoo!"

They both began laughing. "Ah pup, we better just call it a night."

Chapter 3: Running Alone

Sebastian slept well that night, curled up in a ball in his family den. He woke up the next morning fresh and ready to take on the day.

"Hey everybody, I'm just going for a morning run," Sebastian said to his family, who were all still getting up. He stepped out of his den. The sun was just starting to light the sky. This was the favorite part of Sebastian's day—it was dawn. The sky was a periwinkle blue and was quickly getting brighter from the horizon up. The bright starts still appeared low in the sky. Mars and Venus hung like powerful orbs, full of energy and potential. The trees were bare now. It was January so the branches were empty and grey—just a bundle of dry sticks in the brisk air. But Sebastian was warm as he ran through the forest, his thick grey, tan coat a shelter from the wind and biting cold. He had gone running through these woods at dawn many times before. It was invigorating and it made him feel wild, like the coyote he was. Sebastian ran through the maple trees as fast as he could, dodging each tree trunk like a slalom skier. He darted up a steep buckthorn-covered slope, careful not to get tangled in the clumps of twigs.

Sebastian sprinted by oak and birch and ran into a clearing of snow-covered prairie grass—a prairie he had never before been in. This prairie was big and didn't have the same kind of grass and thistle he was used to seeing. This grass was tender, brittle, and long. It crinkled below Sebastian's paws as he sauntered through the tan waves. And before he knew it, Sebastian was walking on clumps of snow and ice. The ghost grey mounds of broken ice were jagged and Sebastian's dull claws and fleshy paws slipped down the smooth faces of frozen, cloudy water. He steadied himself on a chunk and looked out at the eerily swaying mass of water and ice. It was dizzying and mesmerizing and Sebastian felt calm and alone—very very alone. But he didn't feel sad or scared. He felt solitude.

He felt what it was like to be Sebastian and he felt his own breath moving in and out, over his pink tongue that hung hot between his two sharp canine teeth. He felt strong and adventurous, daring and bold. He thought about the words his dad had said the night before, about being himself. And he felt very much like himself right at that moment. With this confidence and pride, Sebastian stomped his right front paw and closed his eyes in a feeling of greatness.

Just then, in that utter silence and terrific energy, a tiny cracking sound emerged from beneath Sebastian's mass. The ice had broken away from the land. Sebastian was teetering on a plank of ice that was now slowly moving into the swaying flow. From above, the scene must have looked like a giant puzzle of ice, each piece turning, twisting, trying to fit into place in slow motion, but one piece bearing a coyote.

To Sebastian, the scene was quite different. It was not slow motion at all, nor was it trying to fit into place. It was confusion. It was panic. It was very fast. Sebastian was moments ago enjoying being alone, and now he was more alone than ever before—drifting. He panted frantically, his tongue waving in and out between his teeth. He paced his ice plank, which was no bigger than his shadow at the end of the day. His heart pounded inside his wide chest cavity and echoed in his ears—it was the only sound—his heart and the panting. Sebastian was slowly floating away from home and it seemed there was nothing he could do.

Sebastian knew he didn't want to run or jump. And no one was around to help—still he howled as his dad had taught him many times, and just the night before. "Whoo Whoo Whoodoooo!" Sebastian cried as loudly as he could, over and over as he moved along the shore. The land was close by but too far away to reach. This frustrated Sebastian and reminded him of when Dominic used to tease him as a young pup by dangling a delicious pheasant in front of him when he was hungry, then pulling it away at the last second.

Sebastian continued to pace his floating ice plank, moving back and forth, back and forth, panting, howling, panting, pacing, looking all along the shore for his mom and dad as he rode by. But all Sebastian saw was grass and trees, and before long he saw steep hills that climbed up to the woods on top and he felt even more alone, down on the lake, in a kind of big hole away from the land. Even if he could get off of the ice now, he never would be able to climb the vertical bluff. But Sebastian couldn't get off of the ice. He was exhausted. He had no choice but to rest, lie down on the ice and watch the land pass slowly by.

The water beneath Sebastian's ice, stretching out to the horizon, was dark grey against the white sky. The mass of water moved together, each motion complementing the other. For every up there was a down. And at the crux of the motion was Sebastian. He was so scared and didn't know how he would ever see his mom, dad, and Dominic again. Every minute he was on the ice he knew he was getting further and further away. What would they think? That he was out contemplating chipmunks again? There was no way they could know where he was and they certainly wouldn't know he'd go out on the ice, out on the lake. What was he going to do?

Sebastian 1/25   H.A. 2003

Chapter 4: Drifting

Sebastian looked up on the bluff above him and he noticed huge mansions on top of the hill. He thought they were too big for one family to live in, but soon realized as he saw mansion after mansion that this was a neighborhood. Sebastian had never seen anything like this before. The grass near the homes was not like the prairie grass near his den—this grass was neat and tidy underneath the dusting of snow. The homes were carefully designed—each one was different and had personality all its own. One home had a large window that overlooked the lake. Inside the home Sebastian could see an ornate chandelier hanging from the cathedral ceiling. A spiral staircase led to the second floor. Another home had three white pillars in front of the red brick structure and looked like a financial institution. Yet another was linear and had beautiful rectangular stained glass windows all over the structure.

The houses were all different but one thing was the same—no one was home. The mansions were all empty and dark inside. Sebastian thought the families who lived in them must be at work, working hard for their home. It made Sebastian miss his family and want to be with them. He knew they were in his den, waiting for him to come back, getting worried. It had been many hours now. Still, Sebastian passed by the land, slowly and steadily.

The bluff up above began to get lower and lower, and soon Sebastian could see taller buildings, growing up toward the winter sky. These buildings looked like they were made of rock. Windows dotted the buildings from the base of the foundation up to the roof. The looming structures made Sebastian feel scared and dark because they were so strange and urban looking. Sebastian felt even more danger. The buildings became more frequent and were closer and closer together—sometimes even touching each other. Above the buildings, plumes of white steam billowed from ventilation ducts into the cold, grey-white sky. Sebastian imagined they were dragons, breathing smoke and fury.

City 7/25   H. A 2004

  And just when he thought he had entered a dungeon, he looked up ahead, at where his ice plank was floating, and saw an immense black silhouette of jagged, pointy buildings jutting up to the sky, looming, calling, moving closer and closer. As the giant mass grew and grew, Sebastian began to see more details of the giant's structure. One tall building even looked like a diamond on top and was lighter in color than many of the others.

  But one shape was so different than everything else—this shape was round and had white lights that raced and chased each other from the center of the circle, out in lines to the perimeter of the circle and back again. Sebastian was mesmerized by the dancing lights as his ice plank moved closer and closer to its luring magic. Sebastian was interested in this contraption and found its energy playful and fun. He started to feel safe again and thought that this new land might be fun. Sebastian could now see the sign that appeared near the circle—it read *Navy Pier Ferris Wheel*.

Sebastian was so intent on watching the light display that he almost didn't notice when his ice plank came to rest among other ice chunks in a nook alongside the great circle. Sebastian was now at rest in the harbor, no longer floating helplessly. The ice was motionless and silent among the hum of car traffic nearby and an ambulance siren in the distance. Sebastian stepped off of his ice block and onto the neighboring chunk of ice and snow, trying hard to keep his balance. He rested for a moment on this plank and looked all around him before the next step. Many of the ice pieces were too small to hold Sebastian's body. Others were plenty big and were stable in the watery soup. Sebastian knew he had to try to leap to the large pieces and make his path to the concrete shore that rose from the lake, only yards away. Sebastian felt he could make it. There was hope. He howled in excitement. He knew if he was brave and skillful he could make it to the shore before sundown. He howled again to let this big city know that he had arrived on its shores and was about to jump into it, alive and wild.

Chapter 5: Water to Earth

Sebastian looked up into the sky. He was used to seeing large fields of open air, framed on the ground by trees. This time he saw metal and glass formed into smooth walls that reached taller than ten oak trees stacked up. Sebastian felt small, like a little pup. Yet he was curious and determined to explore this new experience. Sebastian saw a large piece of ice in front of him that was closer to the breakwater, a pile of concrete rocks in the lake. He sprung toward it using great strength from the muscles in his hind legs, but his power was too much for the distance and Sebastian overshot the ice, landing in the water. Although Sebastian's fur was thick and warm, the icy lake water still penetrated his coat and touched his skin. "Whoo! Whoo!" Sebastian cried from the shock of the cold, and from fear—he had tried so hard to remain calm all the hours he was floating along the north shore, and now that he was almost safe again, he somehow ended up in the lake. Sebastian had never before been in such deep water, only the little river by his family den. His paws couldn't touch the floor of the lake. Yet Sebastian paddled with his front paws, plunking and splashing one and then the other while his back legs kicked steadily in the water. He was staying afloat. His pointy snout was held high in the air, his mouth open and breathing.

Sebastian spotted another large, flat piece of ice only feet away and he propelled himself toward the bloat. He was slowly moving forward. Sebastian was too instinctual to be amazed at his skill—he was only focusing on saving himself. The ice plank was in front of Sebastian and he placed one paw on the edge and then the other, kicking strongly with his hind legs. He used the power of his front arms to pull his chest up out of the lake as his back legs pushed the water fiercely to move his body forward up onto the ice. He slid up and was safe, panting hard from his rescue. The adrenaline started to dissipate in Sebastian's body and he grew calmer on the safety of the ice. Sebastian shook off his thick fur, wiggling quickly from side to side, beginning at the head and moving like a wave throughout his body to his tail. The water flew off of him in a spray, raining into the lake around him.

Sebastian heard the droplets hit the surface of the water and again the harbor was silent, except for the sound of men in the distance.

Sebastian looked up toward the human voices and saw five policemen walking along the shore. "There he is!" one man shouted. They all moved faster now on the shore across from Sebastian. They called to him as if he were a dog. "Here coyote, here coyote!" And they whistled. One man held a long metal rod in his hand. At the end of the rod was a metallic loop. Sebastian didn't know what the contraption was, but he thought, "That can't be good." Sebastian felt he had to avoid the men. Still, he wanted to reach land, and it was getting darker. He didn't want to spend the night on the lake as the temperature dropped. So Sebastian looked for a path to the nearby breakwater. He wanted away from the men, who were still calling to him on the shore as they bent over and slapped their legs to lure him.

"Coyote! Coyote!" Sebastian thought the men were silly, which made him laugh, "Whoooo!" He jumped onto the next slab of ice, then quickly another and another. He was only feet way from the rocks. With all of his strength, Sebastian spring from the ice and the lake and landed first with his front paws and then with his back paws upon the solid rock of the breakwater. Sebastian looked over to the men who were standing on the shore, unable to climb along the wet and snowy rocks that jutted out into the frigid lake and again he let out a "Whoo!" to tell the men he had arrived, was safe, free, and most of all, that he had beat them.

The light was fading from the sky above and care headlights and streetlights and landscaping spotlights and the blinking Ferris wheel lights all began to permeate the scene. Sebastian heard the men speak. "Come on guys, let's hit it— we're not going to catch this guy tonight." When they were in their paddy wagons and cars and gone from the scene, Sebastian jumped easily from rock to rock, running toward the city lights, and moved onto the earth.

Chapter 6: On the Rocks

Sebastian looked down at his paws. His fur was wet and clumped together over his blunt claws. Below his paws were snow and grass and dirt, just as he had left behind near his family den. Sebastian glanced nearby and saw a large metal drum with the words *Property of Chicago Park District* emblazoned in white stenciled paint on its side. Within the drum, Sebastian smelled meat. It wasn't a rabbit or fawn like he was used to, but still, Sebastian was very hungry, hadn't eaten all day, and desperately wanted whatever was inside of the metal drum. Sebastian jumped up onto the edge of the cold drum and rested his front paws on the rim while standing somewhat weakly with his hind legs on the ground—he was hungrier than he thought. Much of his strength until now had come from adrenaline, not stored energy. Sebastian pulled at the drum, toppling it toward him so that he could crawl inside.

From the top of the garbage pile tumbled a white bag with red stripes and letters that spelled *Portillo's*. Sebastian pawed the bag open and found a half-eaten big Italian beef sandwich with sweet peppers and a half order of cheese fries. "How could somebody waste such delicious food?" thought Sebastian. He thought the previous owners of the hearty grub must have been in a hurry or may have been interrupted somehow—still, it didn't matter to Sebastian. He tore into the juice-soaked bread and basil-seasoned beef voraciously. Even though a half of a sandwich was just a snack for Sebastian, there wasn't any more food readily available, and he was very tired from his stressful journey. Sebastian decided to call it a night and scavenge for more food in the morning.

He moved back out along the breakwater, just in case the men came back to capture him, and found a comfortable looking crevasse between two large rocks. He maneuvered into the space and lay down on the flat surface. It was a good shelter from the cold wind off of the lake. But the lights of the city were flashing and shining in Sebastian's face. Even though he tried to put his paw over his snout to shield his eyes, the blinking Ferris wheel lights were distracting and visible. The giant circle loomed over him, larger than any tree or hill he had ever seen. The white lights dotted the spokes of the wheel, pulsing in toward the center, then out to the edge, pulling him in and pushing him out like the waves on the lake that moved against the rock and the shore, tossing bits of debris and rocking the ice shelves. All around Sebastian was motion as he tried to be still and let his exhaustion wash over him into sleep.

But he was alone and afraid and he kept opening his eyes to see if the Ferris wheel was still there or if he was dreaming. He peeked a little to make sure the men weren't approaching with their terrible dog catching contraptions. He peered through a slit in his eyelids to see the motion on the lake and he felt as if he were moving again. Sebastian's pointy ears were alert, cupping the air, waiting for any sounds that would force him to spring into action, but all he heard was the lake water moving in and out of the concrete rocks around him, the dull buzz of car tires on Lake Shore Drive, and ambulance sirens from the emergency room at Northwestern University Hospital. Sebastian just waited, hoping to fall asleep somehow—hoping to block out the distractions that invaded his senses. He realized it would not be long before dawn arrived, and without sleep, he would feel sick and weak.

Somehow, he had to fight off the city and calm his mind. Sebastian pretended he was not on a rock in the lake in a strange city far away—rather, he vividly imagined he was back home, resting on the warm floor of his family den. He imagined the soft crackle of the fallen leaves that blanketed his sleeping area. He saw his mom and dad and Dominic nearby, all curled up like a croissants, snout to tail. He smelled the earthy musk of the den walls—the dirt and the branches carved into the ravine crevasse. He snuzzled his nose into the warm fur of his tail and hind quarters and was safe and sleep.

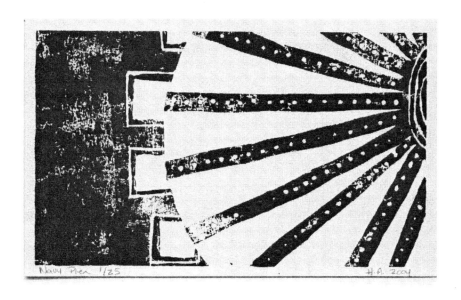

Navy Pier 1/25   H.A. 2004

Chapter 7: Behind Bars

Nearby, the sound of a delivery truck backing up, *beep, beep, beep* woke Sebastian from his short nap. Although he tried to throw his paw over his eyes and snout, the sound was loud and intrusive, slow and rhythmic, and showed no signs of stopping. Sebastian opened one eye to see the familiar rose and periwinkle sky of dawn. Along the far edge of the lake, the sky was light, moving in a gradient of darkness to the sky above. Sebastian could not see Venus and Mars, or the other stars—too much light haze from the city escaped into the sky, obliterating any competing light. Venus and Mars were made invisible by Hancock and Sears.

Sebastian realized that if the sky were becoming brighter, the men with their dog catching contraptions might be back before long to try their skill again. So Sebastian got up from his rock, leaving the spot that had turned warm from his body heat and leapt from rock to rock until he reached land again. To his left he saw many buildings and structures, but to the right was grass and trees. "I think I'll go explore a bit over there by the grass since it reminds me most of home," thought Sebastian. As he trotted along the mixture of grass, concrete, and even some icy sand along the lakefront, Sebastian felt he was experiencing sights and sounds that no one in his family, and none of his friends had ever seen. He was an adventurer. He was bold and strong. He wasn't a little scared pup. "I can take on this city, and heck, if I come across a chipmunk, I bet I could take on that too!" thought Sebastian. "I am in charge!"

Sebastian looked up at the trees around him. They were spaced perfectly apart, every twenty feet or so, and their trunks were draped by a perfect circle of chopped pieces of bark and mulch. These trees were groomed and cared for by hired hands. Still, that didn't stop Sebastian from ignoring his territorial instinct. He walked over to a tall, leafless oak and lifted his leg to claim it, and the surrounding area, as his own.

Lincoln Park   1/25   H. A. 2004

The park was empty and Sebastian felt the cold abandoned air enter his lungs and seep into his body, a large cavernous hollow. He was very hungry. The Italian beef sandwich from last night had now digested and all that was left in Sebastian's stomach was a low rumble. Sebastian knew he had to find more food, but in a park surrounded by concrete and tall building, and in the dead of winter, rabbits and birds weren't abundant. The only bird Sebastian had seen so far was a funny-looking dingy bird that pecked along the ground near the trash can last night. Sebastian though it may have been a dove or a pigeon. Whatever it was, Sebastian thought it would taste like dirt, so he wasn't even tempted to bite it.

Now Sebastian had to be creative and thoughtful about his next meal. He remembered the Italian beef last night and how it was discarded in a garbage can. "Maybe there will be more food in other cans," Sebastian thought. But where would he find another one? Sebastian looked through the open park with his piercing eyes. It was easy for Sebastian to see, in both light and dark, but the sunlight was flooding the grass, and the trees were so sparse. He spotted another large metal drum in the distance, standing near a metal fence. "Maybe that can has something tasty, like meat or more cheese fries," thought Sebastian. So he strode fast and steady over to the can and hunkered down his back in case any other creature threatened his find. The metal drum drew nearer and nearer as Sebastian moved across the frozen ground. When he reached the cold cylinder, Sebastian jumped up, resting his front paws over the barrel's edge and aimed his pointy snout downward into the container. But the drum was empty.

At the thought of having no immediate meal, Sebastian's stomach let out another rumble that echoed deep and low in the void of the garbage can. Sebastian jumped down and looked up into the sky out of frustration and desperation but couldn't be comforted by the dry, skeletal branches of the barren trees. Sebastian was hungry. And he was hungry now! "I don't think I have the energy to continue running through the park, aimlessly looking for garbage cans," thought Sebastian, "especially since I don't even know if there is going to be food inside." A sharp shot of harsh wind blew hard into Sebastian's carcass. He lifted his head and caught the scent of something very familiar, but unexpected—fresh rabbit meat. The wafting smell came from within the metal fence where the garbage can stood. Sebastian noticed a large open gate next to a sign that read "Lincoln Park Zoo." He hunkered down his back once again and moved cautiously with a downward tail toward the delicious scent.

Already Sebastian felt a renewed sense of energy just thinking about eating soon. He propelled himself forward, his paws trouncing steadily on the concrete path, his dulled nails clicking in rhythm. Sebastian concentrated intently on the smell of the rabbit, never noticing the polar bears, seals and cages of hawks. He moved with purpose and determination. The smell grew stronger as he grew closer. He looked up, expecting to find juicy rabbit meat, and he did—lying before him on cold concrete behind a metal cage. But behind the mounds of meat was a creature that surprised Sebastian. It stood calmly, quietly, but somewhat guarded. It too was surprised by what appeared before him. Behind the cage, behind the rabbit meat, stood another coyote.

This coyote was as big as Sebastian's father—tall with a thick neck, full of fur. His coat was coarse and blacker near his tail, but the fur on his belly was white and soft. His muzzle sloped gradually up to his forehead where two yellow eyes stared at Sebastian inquisitively.

Sebastian was the first to speak. "What are you doing in this cage?"

The coyote responded, "I'm in a zoo. That's where we animals live when we're in a zoo—in a cage, in a fenced are, in a tank—so we can't cut loose."

"Doesn't that make you sad?" asked Sebastian.

"Well, I really don't know any other life," said the coyote. "I was born in a zoo in New York City and then moved here to Chicago about a year ago."

Sebastian wanted to continue the conversation, but just couldn't wait any longer. "Say, I am really hungry," said Sebastian. "I came here last night when I accidentally drifted on the lake from up north and I've been looking everywhere for food. I see you have some delicious rabbit there. Do you think you could share some?" asked Sebastian.

The coyote looked down at the mound of meat. "Sure, dawg, take it all if you like. They bring me more chow this evening at 5 p.m. like clockwork. I can do without a little lunch to help out a brother coyote."

With that, the coyote nudged the mound with his snout, pushing the meat through the cage, out onto the concrete where Sebastian stood. Sebastian savagely attacked the flesh, barely breathing as he gulped the savory meal.

"Mmch, thank you, mmch, mmch, so much, mmch, I was so hungry and could only find some Portillo's crumbs last night and this is so delicious," said Sebastian to the coyote as he devoured each morsel in delight.

"Hey, like I said, it's no problem, dawg. We get chow twice a day around here and I always know when and where my next meal is—that's not too shabby of a deal, know what I mean? Sure I'd love to go for a big run like you probably get to do everyday, but I'm used to it here now," said the coyote.

"But don't you ever get bored?" asked Sebastian, taking a quick break from his meal to look up at the coyote out of respect for the conversation and interest in the answer.

"No, not really. Like I said, this is all I know. I'm a creature of habit and I like the routine. Plus, I love seeing the kids and knowing that they're happy when they see me. And if I ever get in the mood for a little action, I just do the pack howl," said the coyote.

"You do what?" asked Sebastian.

"The pack howl," answered the coyote. "You see that hole in the wall over there at the back of my cage? Well that hole leads to my shelter when it gets a little rough out here, like when it rains a lot or when the sun gets to be too much. But the shelter is hollow inside, kinda like a tunnel, and everything inside echoes. So when the zoo keeper comes around the zoo grounds making his rounds, I run inside my hole and just as he passes by, I let out a huge 'whoo whoo whoodooo!' at the top of my lungs. You should see that zoo keeper jump! Because of the echo in the tunnel, he thinks it's a whole pack of coyotes! He runs every time. Every time, I tell ya! Ah, there's no better action than that, dawg!" said the coyote.

Sebastian couldn't help but laugh, "Nsm, nsm, nsm, that's great! What power you have! Say, I didn't even get your name.

Here you gave me your lunch and I don't even know what to call you."

"My name is Canis Latrans Clepticus," said the coyote.

"Geesch," replied Sebastian, "I don't know if I can even repeat that—it's really a mouthful."

"Yeah, I know, but I even have my own sign over there so I learned how to spell it and everything. You can just call me Clepticus if you want," said Clepticus.

"Okay, that seems easy enough. I'm Sebastian. I came from up north and floated here on a plank of ice and I've never been to a city before."

"Well then, Sebastian my friend, you've come to the right city. Chicago is great. The people here are real friendly, the kids are smart and love to learn and play, and there's so much to do here. I'm in a cage all day and still I get to see all kinds of weather from one day to the next, all different types of people from different backgrounds and cultures, there are beautiful buildings all around from all kinds of architects, and as you've even experienced, there are so many wonderful foods here— Italian beef; hot dogs smothered with relish and tomatoes and a slice of pickle; polish sausages heaped with grilled onions and mustard; pork chop sandwiches with the bone still in it—oh dawg, this is a remarkable city. You'll want to call it home in no time. Guess that's why I never get bored, even in this cage— because I'm home. Sweet home Chicago, dawg!"

Just as Clepticus finished his sentence, both coyotes heard a panicked yelling coming from down the concrete path. "Escaped coyote!" shouted a zoo keeper as he ran frantically toward Sebastian. Immediately, Sebastian sprang forward with his strong hind quarters and bolted the same way he came in.

"Thanks for everything Clepticus! You're a real friend!" said Sebastian.

Sebastian knew the zoo keeper thought he belonged in the zoo and Sebastian wasn't about to get stuck living in a cage, even if Clepticus said it wasn't so bad. Sebastian had been born free and lived free and had a whole family and friends waiting for his return up north. So Sebastian ran as fast as he could. He must have been darting at twenty to thirty miles an hour past empty popcorn carts and sno-cone stands. The swimming polar bears were just a blur of white as Sebastian moved past with agility and speed. From the time he was a pup he had learned to dodge trees in the forest as he ran and now he used the same skill to leave the zoo. His paws hit the ground and pulled back up almost immediately with each stride. His ears were keen and alert as he caught the sound "go dawg go" from Clepticus. His fur blew back, sleek and resistant as he bolted down the path like a rocket and passed through the zoo entrance into the park once again.

Chapter 8: Morning Commute

Sebastian stood on the outside of the zoo gate, breathing hard, his pink tongue hanging from his panting mouth as quick puffs of white steam escaped into the chilly air. Even though Sebastian liked talking to Clepticus, and he could tell they would learn a lot from each other, he knew hanging out anywhere near the zoo would only land him in the zoo, so he kept his tail low and moved furtively through the park. He didn't know where he was going—just away.

Across the grass, Sebastian spotted a group of people standing near a three-sided glass hut. Each person was dressed in beautiful clothes and long formal looking coats. Some of them carried bags that likely contained workout clothes, and others held leather bags that probably housed files of documents and laptop computers. Sebastian thought these people must be transporting themselves to work. But Sebastian knew these people weren't doing work like his mom and dad did— constructing additional den space in a crevasse or feeding the family by hunting for rabbits or birds. But still, it probably wasn't all that different—just another form of survival.

As he walked slowly, yet closer to the bus shelter, Sebastian came in from around the rear of the group, who waited, zombie-like, facing the street, watching in the same direction. One woman in black high-heeled boots and a long wool coat wore headphones over her ears to block out the world. She swayed from side to side as the rhythm of the music entered her ears and permeated her soul. A man stood about five feet from the woman and struggled to pull the two sides of his tan trench coat together over his protruding belly. He stared down the road and frequently stepped onto the pavement when the cars went past. He impatiently stretched his neck, looking for the bus, moving his neck up, to the right, back to the left as if spotting the bus would satisfy his frustration. Beads of sweat formed on his balding head even though it was only twenty degrees outside. Another man held a navy blue nylon duffle bag in one hand and peered into a magazine held in the other hand. He held the magazine taut, but occasionally the lake wind would snap the crease from the magazine and the pages would fall limp and flap ferociously. Still, he continued to fight the wind and bury his face, and attention, in the sports pages of his magazine.

No one noticed Sebastian. Sebastian was not a bus or magazine or music, so no one saw him when he sauntered up to a man wearing a long black coat and dark sunglasses, just as the 151 Sheridan bus arrived along the curb, its brakes squealing as it slowed its mass to a halt. As the man moved quickly toward the bus door, which opened like an accordion, Sebastian moved with the man, onto the stair and onto the bus, pausing to slip his transit card into the mechanized fare box and Sebastian slid behind him. The bus driver noticed the man wore dark glasses, saw the animal behind him. The driver pulled on the bus microphone which was attached to the wall with a silver, bendable arm and spoke to the passengers in the front of the bus "Seeing Eye dog, can someone please let us have your seat." By this time, the man in the sunglasses, who paid no attention to the bus driver and was consumed with his own thoughts and his own monotonous routine, had entered the bus and sat in the first open seat. The man was pleased with himself that he could now travel in comfort without standing, hanging like a monkey from one of the overhead poles. Sebastian, or the dog, as the bus driver and passengers now saw him, sat next to the man in the sunglasses in order to perpetuate the Seeing Eye dog myth and to get a free ride. But Sebastian was unable to see out of the bus window since the man was large and engulfed Sebastian's space. So at the next stop, when the bus driver was consumed with his new passengers and their fares, Sebastian jumped from his seat, ran quickly to an open single seat on the right side of the bus, and sprang up with his hind legs, into the upholstered molded plastic seat, aiming his snout toward the window. None of the bus passengers noticed this had happened since they were buried in their Wall Street Journals. Others stared out of their windows too, as if longing for escape. But Sebastian peered through the Plexiglas for different reasons. Sebastian was eager to see all that Clepticus had told

him about. Sebastian wanted to see the great city that was
Chicago, and now he was headed straight into the heart of it.

Chapter 9: Working City

The 151 Sheridan bus sauntered with great weight, bending to the right and left over each buckle of pavement and each pothole. Lake Shore Drive appeared fully visible outside of the windows on the other side of the bus. Only a thin rail of metal separated the bus from the speed of the four lanes along the lake. And then, there was the lake. The water had been dark grey and ominous yesterday while Sebastian floated on top of it, drifting at the mercy of the water's motion. Today the lake was deep blue and still against the quiet, windless sky. No one on the bus saw the early morning serenity. No one experienced the unusually peaceful scene as the bus meandered down the inner drive. No one looked at the flatness of the great liquid mass that somehow satisfied any fear or worry. No one except Sebastian.

He turned his attention back to buildings of concrete, the tops of which could not be seen from his bus window. As the bus made a stop at Division Street, Sebastian glimpsed a building covered by a metal scaffold. Men dotted the scaffold like bees on a comb of honey as dust flew into the air and the piercing sound of a concrete saw invaded the bus. The men on the scaffold wore dark blue jump suits that were swarmed with fine grey soot, goggles with orange tinted lenses and white masks over their noses and mouths.

On the sidewalk below, a woman walked on tall heels, exited through the building's revolving door, and entered her day at a desk, her lanky, wrinkled body covered by a two-thousand dollar navy blue Channel suit and a fine cashmere wrap. She extended her braceletted arm along the curb, hailed a cab, climbed inside, and disappeared.

The bus lurched forward jerkily and moved along the inner drive, traveling past the cobblestone mansions, constructed during a long-ago Chicago era. Surely the faces inside had changed, but the wealth and the names had not. The American dream had been realized decades ago and was now kept by the lucky few. Soon the bus entered the Mag Mile. "Michigan

Avenue" read the street signs, and Sebastian saw store windows sparsely decorated with expensive clothes, handbags, and shoes.

Sebastian was intrigued and curious about these temples of extravagant goods, but his staring eyes were suddenly caught by the motion of a figure walking swiftly past the luxurious panes of glass. His instantaneous reaction to the moving figure was one of uncanny comfort. But when Sebastian focused on the moving mass, his comfort turned to horror as he recognized the pelt of his fellow beaver stretched and sewn into a coat, draped over the body of an obese old woman in boots. "Mmmp!" Sebastian let out an uncontrollable reaction from deep in his throat, his mouth still shut in horrified awe. No one on the bus had heard or seen Sebastian's discomfort as they read their books and magazines within the comfort and safety of their imagined barriers. Sebastian's wet black nose smudged the cold bus window as he stared closer at the huge woman, trying hard to see the face of this creature who now wore the skins of his friends like a trophy.

Sebastian thought of the Botteghe family, a large clan of beavers he and his brother knew down by the ravine. Sebastian visualized them working to build a larger hut, chewing through wood with great skill and speed, and patting mud into place. He remembered the time Gio Botteghe, the youngest boy in the family, spotted a couple of hunters coming through the woods with their flashy orange hats and their long cold guns. So Gio, relying on his strength and the adrenaline coursing through his body, womped his flat, skillet-like tail as hard as he could on the surface of the creek, alerting the entire Botteghe family to flee. The beavers that now adorned the body of the gargantuan, gluttonous woman weren't as lucky as the Botteghe family that day. As slow as the bus moved down Michigan Avenue, it was still too fast for the beaver-adorned woman who waddled, out of breath, and soon she was out of Sebastian's sight.

Above the bus towered a dark metal structure, stemming from the concrete ground, crisscrossing like the legs of a water strider on the surface of a smooth reflective pond, up and up and

up, further than Sebastian's nose could see. A sign on the
concourse of the great monolith read "Hancock Building," as
residents filed out and workers filed in, spinning through
quartered circular doors of glass and steel. Next to the immense
metal structure was a square building that was silent in the early
morning, but Sebastian could sense the frenzy that would soon
begin within the cold stone walls of Water Tower Place.

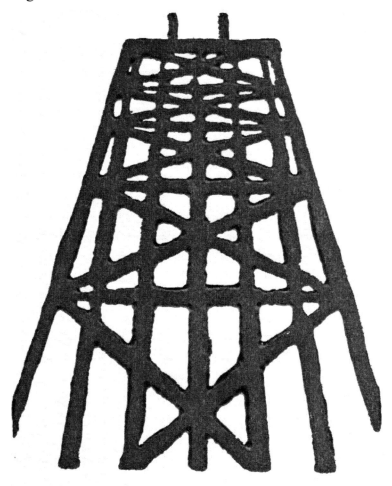

1/25   Hancock   HMA

The bus moseyed forward down Michigan Avenue as passengers repeatedly pulled a wire that rang a bell, telling the bus driver to let them off at the next stop. Sebastian heard the ringing and detected the movement of the passengers, but his gaze out of the scratched Plexiglas window was unaffected. He was completely in awe of this strange civilization. Portly white-haired men in suits and black wool trench coats walked next to sinewy boys with bike helmets, florescent orange messenger bags, and fingerless gloves. Women with pulled and painted faces teetered on stiletto heels and carrying Birken bags next to teenage girls with Burger King and McDonalds hats over gelled, pony-tailed hair. Everyone was headed to work. They were walking to their desks up in the sky, their French fry baskets, their bicycles, their jackhammers on Lower Wacker, their bridge tender houses, their mop buckets, their telephones and computers, their X-ray machines and CAT scans, their radar screens with the blips of airplanes, their ticker tape, their pipes and wrenches, their hard hats and blueprints, their press releases, their saltimbocca chicken and zucchini fritti, their squeegees and ropes, their blow torches, their paint brushes, their hammers, their pens. This was a working city.

Chapter 10: In the Loop

Sebastian had come to Chicago floating on a piece of ice. Now he was moving through Chicago, into the center of the action on a bus. He was nearing the Loop. One block away, Sebastian could hear the rumbling and the clatter of the El, a train that moved with speed, sparking along steel tracks on wooden lifts. Within the train, more workers transported themselves to their jobs. Within the walls of each building, workers moved up in elevators and escalators. Cars gradually crept forward in the lanes next to the bus, entering underground tunnels to rest as the cars' inhabitants climbed up stairwells into the surface of the city. All around there was movement back and forth, up and down, in and out. Sebastian had once heard of this phenomenon—the Rat Race. It was humorous how humans lived. It wasn't so different from the bees or ants or squirrels that Sebastian saw everyday. Still, Sebastian observed in amazement at the scene.

Sebastian now noticed that the people walking on the sidewalks and crosswalks here in the belly of the beast were moving together, in packs, like one big mass. As the bus stopped before Madison Avenue, a hoard of professionals in long wool coats carrying leather laptop bags stepped off of the concrete curb in both directions and headed toward each other like jousting knights on horses. Instead of clashing with a metal clang, the two briskly-moving clans passed through each other gracefully, as if they were ghosts, and reformed together on the other side as a solid mass. Sebastian didn't know how they did it. Even he and his friends had never traveled in such a way. At first, seeing the power of these enormous moving mobs made Sebastian feel anxious, but then it suddenly hit him. He could go unnoticed through these streets. The mobs moved with too much purpose to take notice of an anomaly such as a coyote. But where would he like to go? What would he like to see?

The bus crept along Michigan Avenue, inching its way behind a line of endless busses in the right lane, creaking to a stop at each traffic light and every bus stop. Outside the bus window, two greenish lions stood guard over a pale-colored building. The lions were majestic. Proud kings of the city. Suddenly, the bus turned onto a street marked *Adams*. Sebastian didn't know where the bus was headed, but he didn't feel worry or discomfort since he knew he would exit soon, amid the hoards of walkers. As the bus passed underneath the El track, a train traveled perpendicular overhead. The clash of the train's metal wheels on the steel rails sounded like a collision and Sebastian lost the control of his own thoughts. Panic distracted Sebastian and he let out an instinctual "whoo whoo whoodoo!" but no one on the bus heard. Sebastian's howl was drawn out by the rolling, pounding weight of the El.

When the train cars had passed, and the bus continued west, Sebastian shook his head briefly from side to side, trying to shake away the disorienting experience. He knew the city would be overwhelming the minute he viewed its towering landscape from afar on his ice drift, but he had no idea the sensation of having the city invade and take control of his senses and mind. Sebastian felt he was merely a visitor here now. He was not in charge, but was at the mercy of the power of the urban metropolis. He could never begin to understand all that took place within these streets, buildings, and tunnels, but respected the beauty of its activity—the dance and balance of people and their constructs—their systems and energy. Sebastian's panic became pride. He was proud to be a part of this carefully crafted life. He was an observer, but for the first time, he felt he was also a participant.

Chapter 11: Cacophony

The droves of workers grew bigger as the bus entered the heart of the financial district. Sebastian could see inside the lobbies of the buildings as they passed. They were smooth, shiny lobbies, sparsely decorated to convey the frugal and responsible companies housed within. Or at least, that's how they appeared. One building had four Greek-looking columns of Indiana limestone supporting the outside entrance, two on each side of a set of revolving doors, through which was a bank of security desks and turnstiles freed only by a magnetically-coded name badge. Another building had panes of dark reflective glass that sloped away from the street at a 45 degree angle until it shot straight up into the sky like a laser beam, cool and electric. The bus stopped, then moved, stopped, then moved. Yellow taxis darted in front of the bus, horns blared as the bus ambled like a swimming whale. The bus moved into the path of oncoming Range Rovers and Cherokees, each inhabited by a single person—the driver. Sebastian's attention was distracted from the chaos outside the bus by voices two seats behind him. With the exception of the external noise, the ringing of the stop bell, and the automated voice declaring the next stops, the bus, until now, had been silent. Protective barriers prevented conversation. But a young woman and a young man, each wearing over-stuffed nylon and aluminum backpacks, spoke with heavy British accents about their stop that was nearing.

"I think the entrance is on Jackson Booolevod," said the woman, her hair wrapped loosely in a messy ponytail.

The man replied, "Yeah, the book says the Calder sculpture is in the lobby there and the lift to the Sky Deck is there as well."

"Well, I don't see it yet, but I feel like we're just upon it," said the woman.

An older woman sitting across the bus aisle from the couple felt compelled to come out of her protective shell. "You guys looking for the Sears Tower?" They nodded with a smile.

"She's on that corner—get out at this stop," and the older woman reached up with her gloved hand and pulled the plastic-coated wire cord for the two.

"Thank you, ma'am," said the young man as they both twisted their torsos to brace the weight of their packs. They got up from their seats and started for the narrow back door as the bus moved toward the curb.

"The next stop is Wacker. Wacker Boulevard is the next stop," said the automated announcement from the speakers of the bus. A digital display above the driver's window spelled "WACKER" in red dots that scrolled over and over from right to left. The bus slowed and Sebastian made his move, bolting quickly from his window seat to the floor. He heard the same woman who had helped the backpackers gasp as Sebastian moved with stealth toward the back door. The bus stopped and the green light above the back doors lit, indicated the doors were freed for exit. Sebastian slinked toward the heels of the backpackers, and as they pushed open the doors, he moved like a shadow. Suddenly, the older woman on the bus cried out, "Oh my God, there's a stray dog!" The few business men and women left on the bus looked up, perhaps more surprised at the fact that someone had spoken rather than the actual words that came out of her mouth. Sebastian didn't know what reaction the people on the bus had as they glimpsed his furry tail escape from the back door. He was out of the bus. He was on the sidewalk, surrounded by tall buildings and hurried traffic.

Sebastian moved to an unused delivery door that created an alcove in the building directly across the sidewalk from him. Here he could sit unnoticed, out of the hustle and bustle of pedestrians as he collected his thoughts and planned his next move. Cigarette smoke curled into Sebastian's alcove from a puffing man standing near the bus stop. He stood with two other smoking women. They all chatted like birds, chirping about their day in the workplace that was about to begin. The shops along the street were closed—too early for shopping. A suit and tie store boasted an *annual sale* sign in its window but Sebastian sensed it wouldn't be any busier later in the day than it was right now. It was January, the hardest month of the year for a suit and tie store named *Nick's*. Next door was an office supply store with a small display of reams of copy paper and stacks of file folders that cost twice as much as the chains. But this was the price of convenience and with this inflation many staff employees and the owner could pay off their student loans and medical bills.

The street lights—their new construction but old design— the rows of newspaper boxes, red, dark blue, plastic yellow, metal white—they all stood still in the middle of the motion—the cars on one side—delivery trucks from FedEx and Phillip's Flowers and Coffee Unlimited—white vans with ladders on top, and Kitty Kat Tour busses, and American United Taxis, daredevil bike messengers with helmets and bags full of boxes—bankers in suits under cashmere coats, traders in Kelly green or yellow or teal cotton blazers under barn jackets from the Gap and J. Crew, their plastic identification badges clipped to the outside fabric— women in black heels and long dresses and taupe nylons stretched over chilly legs, carrying lattes, skim milk, no foam, sprinkled with cinnamon—lawyers with leather, box-like cases, piled one on top of the other, pulled by thin metal luggage carriers—cell phones and more cell phones—the sound of the El grew and faded—truck guts boomed as the bumpy pavement rattled the loosed metal with speed—CTA bus brakes screeched and screeched as the passengers inside jolted forward with each press of the pedal—horns of cabs gave a *toot* to show impatience at slow moving street crossers or they held the horn for a long, rage-filled sound to signify anger at a car's stopped motion—car tires sounded like blowing wind as they picked up brief speed on the pavement, their radio's rhythm loud and pounding. All of it flowed like a choreographed dance.

Sebastian felt overwhelmed. He was sure there were such comings and going near his home. Sap crawled up into the branches of the maples and oaks and spread nourishment to the thirsty buds; rain melted the mud on the daubers home; acorns transformed into wood; sunlight from blinding to shadow passed over frozen ground; insects hollowed the trunks of trees, year after year until all that remained was reddish power; the deer gave birth; the wolf spider snared her meal in a grassy trap; the male cardinal dropped a red feather to the ground, found by a child on a hike at Camp Meadowbrook; tree frogs laid their eggs in standing water and tadpoles swam until they bloomed L-shaped legs; clouds curled and unfurled; soil shifted; fish ate smaller fish; bees served the queen in the comb; grasses flourished and dug in deep; water striders slid on water as if it were glass; the ground froze and thawed, the seasons passed into one another; fire, water, air, and earth moved in balance and discord. Sebastian lived among these systems, these occurrences, every day and so they were not so strange. But out here in the morning streets of the city, Sebastian felt uneasy, disoriented, and on his own.

Chapter 12: Disrupting the Motion

Sebastian stood on the cold pavement, his four paws firm on the surface. He was reminded of his night on the breakwater as the chill of the sidewalk seeped into his bones. He had to get moving again, to keep warm, and he was curious about this Sears Tower he had heard about on the bus. If travelers came from around the world to see this famous structure, Sebastian wanted to take advantage of his visit to Chicago and see what the fuss was all about. He knew the great building was just across the street, and that the crowds didn't seem to be thinning as time went on, so Sebastian entered the storm. As Sebastian stepped into the flow of people, he carefully judged their speed and maintained the same stride. Again, he was adrift in a lake, moving with the clicking heels of leather boots and stomping of finely-crafted Oxfords wrapped in the rubber covers of galoshes. Sebastian hunkered low and undetectable beneath the glazed-over gaze of the walkers. He walked down the block over black slush and metal grates from which came a warm, smelly blast of air.

Sebastian couldn't see from inside the group of walkers, but he was already alongside of the Sears Tower. He could sense the energy of the huge beast towering above him, around him. He could hear the sounds of car horns and tires on pavement and bus engines hit the face of the great giant and then bounced back into the vortex of activity. It was loud here. Up above, the clouds covered the sun, thick and impenetrable.

The monolith of glass and steel shielded the diffused light emitted by the sky and the building surrounding Sebastian pulled him into the black hole and pushed back the light. It was dark and heavy, moving in the hoard among the massive structures. Sebastian felt engulfed. He saw through the legs of the pack and glimpsed a door just opening along the massive foundation of the Sears Tower. Through the door came a man in a FedEx uniform with a dolly of stacked boxes in his hands. Nearby spun a revolving door of the walkers, moving with speed and agility into the motion of the glass and steel, disappearing on the other side.

Sears Tower 1/25   H.A. 2004

"I don't think I can navigate that spinning door. It looks like a blender," thought Sebastian. "And even if I could, I sure couldn't stay secret for very long." Sebastian quickly assessed the situation. "I'll have to jump quickly through the side delivery door," he thought. Instinctually, Sebastian supplied adrenaline to his body and exited the pack. He sprung toward the open door. As the FedEx delivery man maneuvered his dolly through the open door, Sebastian slipped in under the radar just before the door clamped shut. The FedEx man never even saw Sebastian, nor felt his wind since the man was covered from head to toe in a warm winter uniform.

Standing on the other side of the entrance, Sebastian immediately surveyed his surroundings. He saw a stream of workers file like ants through the revolving door, each headed toward a security desk and flashed an ID badge at a computerized sensor panel that released a turnstile for their entry into the workplace. The workers in line were consumed with juggling their laptop bags, newspapers, and cups of coffee while fishing around in purses and pockets for their ID badges. Sebastian knew this presented an opportunity. If he could time the movement of the line properly, he could sprint through the turnstile under the nose of the security guards and go undetected by the moving workers. "I'm going to have to move quickly since I'm still in plain view to all of the people at the entrance," thought Sebastian.

He watched the workers moving through the turnstile and as the next one was on deck, ready to move forward, Sebastian jumped forward with his hind legs and sped toward the opening between the turnstile and the workers' approaching legs. Sebastian entered the space and slid through the turnstile opening, but one worker's leather oxford shoe stepped on Sebastian's tail that hung low and close to the ground. Sebastian reacted without thinking, letting out a loud, "Whoo whoo!" that echoed through the marbled lobby. Sebastian immediately snapped up his tail which then got caught above him in the mechanism of the turning turnstile bars. Again Sebastian screamed "whoo whoooo!" and silence washed over the entire entrance. All of the workers stopped in their routine paths and turned their eyes to the direction of the unusual noise. Everyone—the workers, the security guards, the delivery people, CEOs, maintenance staff, shop owners, secretaries—everyone was silent, motionless, and staring straight at Sebastian. He instinctively turned back to look at his tail. Seeing it was not caught in the turnstile, Sebastian lurched forward and sprinted through the marble lobby, past the colorful Caulder mobile, past hundreds of silent, motionless people paralyzed with fear, and bolted toward the elevator bank.

In an instant, Sebastian saw his escape. An elevator car waited as if it were just for him—doors open and inviting—a welcoming shelter from the chaos. Sebastian flung himself into the elevator car and stood, panicked, waiting for the doors to close and leave the danger behind. But the doors did not close. Sebastian paced the small car, staring at the door opening, hoping he would not see people emerge to capture him. He expected to soon see the metal contraption held by the men on the lake, but suddenly, the two elevator doors slowly approached each other. The gap was closing. The danger was disappearing. The panic was fading. Until Sebastian realized, he had no idea where he was going.

Chapter 13: Into the Sky

The metal cage rose with a glimmer of a shake, slowly at first, then speeding up and shaking more. Sebastian was hurtling toward the unknown. The velocity and trembling of the floor beneath his four paws only made matters worse. Without warning, a deep man's voice came over the elevator speaker.

"In only three minutes, you will be entering the Sears Tower Skydeck—an experience like no other," said the voice. "Right now you are climbing one-quarter of a mile into the sky over the City of Big Shoulders—Chicago, home to the tallest building in North America. Standing 110 stories tall and 1,450 feet high, the Sears Tower boasts views of Michigan, Illinois, Indiana, and Wisconsin. On a clear day, you can see 40 to 50 miles in any direction. Built in 1973 by the architectural firm of Skidmore, Owings, and Merrill, the Sears Tower cost over $150 million to build. It is made of enough concrete to build a highway eight lanes wide and five miles long, and it has enough steel to make 50,000 automobiles, and enough telephone wire to wrap around the globe almost twice," continued the voice.

Sebastian might have been amazed at the information booming through the elevator speaker, but he was simply too scared to concentrate on anything but the doors in front of him. He knew that the doors would soon part, slide open, and he would have to immediately respond. He couldn't plan. He couldn't imagine what he would see. Sebastian was filled with anxiety and paced the trembling floor of the elevator. His tail hung down low, his head was crouched and ready to react, his ears were perked to receive, and his nose started to detect that people were near. The elevator slowed and the voice returned to the speaker.

"We have now arrived at the Sears Tower Sky Deck. Please disembark to your right and enjoy the sky." The elevator car stopped and the doors parted. Sebastian heard the sounds of people talking, but sensed they weren't immediately close. With caution, Sebastian stepped out of the car and onto the blue carpet as if he were stalking a rabbit on a ground full of leaves. As

Sebastian emerged from his capsule, he saw the Sky Deck was full of exhibits, each giving more information about the immense structure and the sights below. Buttons and speakers and lights dotted the colorful surfaces of the interactive displays. Sebastian thought they would make great shelters from the people walking among them. He could shield himself from the tourists and plan his next move. Or maybe, he could even "enjoy the sky," as the voice in the elevator told him. After all, Sebastian was curious about the view and he wondered if he might be able to see home.

Sebastian walked carefully on the soft blue carpet and moved with stealth behind the tall laminated structures to the panes of glass that stood floor to ceiling. He pressed his wet black nose to the window and stood in awe of what lay below. Surprisingly, he was not at all frightened. He was thrilled. Patches of buildings separated by lines of concrete covered every inch of ground beneath the brilliant monolith. Puffs of white smoke from the tops of buildings looked like tiny cotton balls below. Sebastian spotted Lincoln Park, the large strip of brownish-whitish grass that held the empty garbage cans and the home of Clepticus.

Just to the north of that strip, Sebastian could see an area, so tiny, but so distinctively a baseball diamond, and he recognized that this was the playground of the famous Chicago Cubs. Sebastian had seen photos in newspapers his father collected to help pad the family den. Sebastian couldn't wait to tell his dad he saw the Friendly Confines from such a spectacular perspective. The small structure lay along the path of a paved line—a street—that cut through the sea of buildings and street lights whose poles staked its claim. Sebastian turned his snout away from the window to the sign beside him. He saw, from the colorful map, that this street was Clark Street—a diagonal thoroughfare up the city's north side. As far as Sebastian could see, the city buildings spread north to the end of the horizon. Sebastian was terrified to see how far away his home was— beyond the horizon, beyond his view, even from a quarter mile into the sky. He felt empty, isolated, and missed the comfort and familiarity of his home. Only five minutes ago he wanted to explore the great unseen sights of the Sears Tower, but now he just wanted to curl up in his family den, close his eyes, and listen to the snoring of his father in the hollow of the ravine.

Chapter 14: The Evil Within

Sebastian sat on his hind quarters, lost in his thoughts of home and waves of anguish and solitude. But his thoughts were distracted by the constant murmur of people talking nearby. "What are those mumbling voices?" Sebastian wondered to himself. Sebastian's attention then immediately jolted back to the moment. "I have to stay alert at what is going on here, or else I might get caught—I'm not safe yet." Sebastian tuned into the voices that sounded hushed and plotting. Instead of instinctually fleeing, Sebastian was curiously drawn to the sounds. Sebastian sensed something was strange and he slinked along the north windows of the Sky Deck, toward the talking men, although he could not yet see them.

Moving to the corner of the observation deck, an enormous silver space ship set like a dish into the top of a classical-looking building lined with Grecian columns caught Sebastian's attention. He had to know what this alien invasion was, in case he should have to run for cover from an approaching infestation of extraterrestrials. The sign to Sebastian's back told him the monstrosity was Soldier Field, home to the Chicago Bears football team, designed by the grandson of the famous architect Ludwig Mies van der Rohe. Sebastian wondered what Mr. Mies van der Rohe would think of his family legacy since this space ship only resembled the master's work with the materials used, but in little else. Sebastian diverted his eyes from the metal toilet bowl and continued slinking toward the luring, moving voices, like a sailor drawn upon the rocks by sirens. He moved along the face of the east side of the deck, along the shore of the lake. A sign revealed that Meigs Field, a small private air strip, had once stood along the lakefront. Government dignitaries, presidents, even royalty had landed upon this runway that was clandestinely destroyed for controversial and conflicting reasons, read a sign. Sebastian was happy to see that a park now stood in its place instead of the high rise development like the ones that blanketed the rest of the city.

The voices stopped their movement on the west side of the Sky Deck. Sebastian sensed the voices were very near now so he took cover behind a glossy exhibit wall that gave information about the cultural attractions of the Museum Campus and the south side. In a foot of space underneath the exhibit, Sebastian saw the feet of the two plotting men. Their feet were covered in shiny, polished, fine leather shoes, brushed gently by the pressed cuffs of Italian suit pants. Sebastian could see these were serious, important men—but who were they and what were they scheming? Sebastian heard their conversation better now that he was so close to them, but he was well hidden and felt safe. Their words started to take shape and Sebastian heard with clarity.

"Is it one of these buildings here on the lake?" a deep voice asked.

"No," replied a whisper, "it's down there, beyond those buildings—that's Hyde Park. See that wide beige building straight ahead along Lake Shore Drive?" he asked.

"Before the Midway, or after the Midway?" the low voice asked.

"Before the Midway, on the north side of it, right there," he replied.

"Ah, yeah, I see it now—that's the Museum of Science and Industry, eh? What a beauty," came the low whisper.

Sebastian peered up at the sign that served as his camouflage and saw the words Museum of Science and Industry above his head. The exhibit revealed that the building that housed the current museum is the only remaining structure from the 1893 Columbian Exposition. The sign said that the building was called the Palace of Fine Arts during the Exposition and was built in 1892, designed by Charles Atwood. Countries from all over the world contributed over 8,000 pieces of art from the likes of Auguste Renoir, Winslow Homer, and Mary Cassatt that were housed in the building's 140 rooms. The building sat on the north bank of the North Pond among the other international buildings. But all of the other great structures from the World's Fair had since been torn down—all except for the Palace of Fine Arts, which was now the Museum of Science and Industry on Lake Shore Drive and 57th Street in Hyde Park.

Sebastian listened in to the two strange men.

"Well the front of the museum property is where she's held, down below the ground," one of the men said in a quiet, sneaky voice.

Sebastian wondered who "she" was. Could it be a person or an animal? Who was below the ground? He listened carefully.

"She used to be outside, along the back of the building, but now they've moved her inside, below the front yard, to protect her from the harsh Chicago weather—especially with the lake right there," and the man pointed out of the left window.

Now Sebastian understood what they were talking about. He remembered that boats are always referred to as a "her" or a "she" and he looked up at the sign again to see a photo of what was below the ground. It was massive and stretched from one end of the museum to the other. How could it ever have once moved beneath the waves, secretly gliding during World War II, carrying hundreds of German soldiers until it was discovered and captured off the coast of Africa, brought years later to the shores of Chicago for all to see? This was the U505 submarine. The U Boat. The Sub. Sebastian wondered why the men were so interested in the tons of steel and what they were planning. He cupped his ears to hear every word.

"Now that she is below the ground, it makes our job a lot easier," said the man. "Or should I say, your job," he continued.

"What do you mean?" questioned the other man.

"Well, first of all, you'll be shielded from the public, so with the exception of the security guards, you'll have secrecy to work with your team. Plus, and this is the most important part, and why my boss is paying you so well for your expertise as a Deep Tunnel engineer—you are close to one of the Deep Tunnel entrances. We've studied the maps and understand that an entrance to the system is located within the new chamber housing the Sub," he whispered.

"You're right," replied the other man—the engineer. "I remember when that section of the Deep Tunnel was added. We had to be careful and take extra precautions because of the lake being so close by—we didn't want to flood the whole system and ruin decades of work, and do damage to the whole city, so we had to add a special wall along the east side of the tunnel for protection. I was in charge of that phase of the Deep Tunnel construction. I know every nook and cranny down there. Heck, I practically lived down there for a year or two. My wife saw me so little, she used to call me the groundhog," said the engineer.

"We know," said the man. "I mean about your involvement, not about the groundhog thing." They both chuckled. "But anyway, my boss, who, of course, shall remain nameless, knows about your experience and expertise, and, if I may be so bold, your love of money to support your many vacation homes and your penthouse on Oak Street. So that is why you have been chosen to lead our little project as well," said the man. "We think that you will agree that the sum of money being offered for the completion of this task will convince you that you are needed and we think everyone will be happy with the outcome. Well, everyone except the locals and tourists, but they are what we'll call a non-factor here—not important," finished the man, and they both gave a few guttural chuckles.

"Well, I must say, you've definitely peaked my interest," said the engineer.

"We thought we would," replied the man with a note of energy in his whispering voice. "Here's what we would like you to do," he continued. "We need you to assemble a team—only you know who you can trust and who can accomplish the great task at hand. Then we would like you and your team to disassemble the Sub—however necessary, but not to cause any damage, because, after all, it will need to be reassembled. Then piece by piece, you and your team will move the Sub down through the entrance of the Deep Tunnel where you will transport it to an undisclosed location exactly five miles away, hoist up the parts, and put the Sub back together as it once was."

The engineer couldn't help by emit a shocked, loud response. "What!? Are you crazy?!" he bellowed.

"Shhhh!" said the man. "Keep your voice down. This is extremely sensitive information we're discussing here. Before you decide and react again, let me tell you what we have to offer."

There was a pause, as if to clear the air.

"We are prepared to supply all equipment necessary—any pulleys, lifts, hydraulics, modes of transportation, joists, welding materials, blow torches, etcetera. We don't know much about this sort of thing—that's your area of knowledge, so you tell us and we will obtain whatever necessary to complete the job. And we'll get it immediately too. We have sources. And when the task has been carried out, and the Sub has arrived intact at its new location, then and only then will you and your team receive payment. The payment we are prepared to offer is," and again the man paused to clear the air and for effect, "is fifty million dollars."

The engineer audibly gasped, which was followed by another "shhhh" from the other man.

"Sorry," whispered the engineer, "I just don't understand why anyone would pay so much money and I have to ask—why the Sub? What does your bass want with the U Boat?"

The man responded, "Well, I really can't discuss anything about my boss. Let's just say, he is an acquirer of fine things and a bit of a history buff and he has had his eye on the Sub for many years. Only recently has he learned of the Deep Tunnel's location beneath the new Sub exhibit and began to consider the possibilities of having the wonderful beauty for his own, to enjoy all of the time, to covet, to own."

"But," interrupted the engineer, "can't he just go look at it anytime he wants? You know, buy a membership or something. Right now so many other admirers can enjoy it too."

"Remember," said the man, "the others, as you call them, are not important here. My boss finds value, value to the tune of $50 million, to calling the vessel his own, and we must not be swayed by removing it from the others who look at it too. They are, as I said, non-factors in this equation. They simply don't matter. What matters is, are you in or not?"

The engineer didn't even take a second to respond. "Yeah, of course, I'm honored to be chosen. I'm definitely in. Consider it done. Now, let's get to work."

Chapter 15: The Tunnel Plan

Sebastian heard the two men walk away, their hard leather-bottom dress shoes clicking on the tile. Sebastian wondered what the Deep Tunnel was—this passageway where they would transport the stolen U505 Submarine, piece by piece. Sebastian looked around at the informative signs surrounding him. There, near the northeast windows, stood a sign with a photo of a tunnel. Above it were the words *Metropolitan Water Reclamation District of Greater Chicago and the Reversal of the Chicago River*. Sebastian quickly trotted unnoticed over to the sign. He skimmed past the paragraphs on the addition of the locks to the mouth of the Chicago River, down past the information on diverting the river's flow from Lake Michigan to the rivers downstream, to the text that surrounded the photo of the large, darkly lit tunnel.

The paragraph was titled *Tunnel and Reservoir Plan— TARP*. "Could this be the Deep Tunnel the men spoke of?" Sebastian wondered. It had to be, he thought. Sebastian read that the tunnels began in the 1970s, built by engineers to stop flooding and water pollution during times of great rain. In order to prevent raw sewage overflow from entering the river system, the Deep Tunnel could be opened to hold the raw water until a time when it could be treated and re-introduced into the system. The sign said that the Deep Tunnel was opened in 1985 with the first 31 miles and that more tunnels are being constructed everyday. There were currently about 51 miles of Deep Tunnel burrowed some 200 to 300 feet below ground and 131 miles of tunnel have been planned for the whole system. Sebastian knew that the El train ran underground in parts of the city through tunnels, but he had no idea there was another set of tunnels even further below the city's tall buildings, slithering like a serpent, insidious and surreptitious.

Sebastian looked out of the window, across the vast lake. For the first time, he wasn't looking at the water thinking of home—he was thinking of the tunnels that carried the water, and the U Boat on the water and those people that the to men called *non-factors*—the ones who weren't *important*. Sebastian had only been in the city for a short time, but he knew the people who lived here and the people who came to appreciate its offerings weren't *non-factors*. They were important. Sebastian thought about how many people went to the Museum of Science and Industry to see the U Boat and how many would never see it again if these men got their way. From the newspapers on his family den's floor, Sebastian had read about thieves stealing great masterpieces of art from museums and galleries, never to be appreciated again by the public. And Sebastian thought that this was exactly the same thing. These two men were thieves, stealing a piece of art, in many ways, that is appreciated by many. He knew he could not let these thieves get away with their plan. He looked out at the lake again and imagined the U Boat arriving on Chicago's shore, coming to rest at the museum. "I am going to make sure that the museum is where the Sub will stay," thought Sebastian. "I will make sure of it."

Chapter 16: The Descent

Sebastian set out to save the Sub, knowing he was the only one in the city who was aware of the thieves plan. If he got caught, not only would he risk never seeing his family again, he would risk the city never seeing the Sub again. He had to be stealth, quieter than ever, sneakier than ever, and more successful than ever. This was no chipmunk he was chasing down a hole. This was the biggest heist going down the biggest and deepest hole in the city. Still, Sebastian was determined to save the Sub, so he decided he wouldn't waste one more minute and leave the Sears Tower right away.

Knowing there were guards by the elevators, and that more and more people would be coming up to the observation deck as the morning grew late, Sebastian looked for a door to the stairwell. Even though he was 110 stories up in the sky, going down stairs couldn't be that hard, he thought, and they certainly would be more secretive than a tourist elevator in one of the most popular attractions in the city. He sighted a door just feet away from him along the wall in the center of the deck. He crouched down with his snout parallel to the ground and saw no feet or legs in his path or nearby. So Sebastian crawled like a sniper underneath the signs in his approach to the door and easily made it, jumped up with his front paws to push the metal bar, and entered the stairwell without incident. He immediately began trotting down the concrete stairs, his thick claws clicking like an old-fashioned typewriter used by a skilled secretary.

At the bottom of each flight, Sebastian would have to turn to continue the flight in the other direction where a door to the next floor appeared. "Wait a minute," Sebastian thought. "This means there are two flights per floor!" and having to change direction by turning each corner for every floor, Sebastian soon found he was using a lot of energy. And the fluorescent lights against the drab grey of the concrete and metal didn't help Sebastian feel inspired to overcome his immense task. But the larger responsibility of preventing the thieves from taking Chicago's treasure motivated Sebastian to press on. His legs continued to move with rapidity and were a blur as he bounced from stair to stair. He began panting heavily. The air was stale. Sebastian's stomach growled as he used his last bits of energy to escape the tower. "What floor am I on now? How much further?" he wondered. He glanced up at the door as he turned the railing for the next flight. *62* said the spray painted stencil on the door. Sebastian wished he hadn't seen it. He was only about half way down. He just didn't think he could do the rest of the stairs without a rest, some food, and water. But there wasn't any time for any of that, if he wanted to stake out the thieves at the museum. They had cars and could move quickly without notice. Sebastian had to walk and could be spotted and caught at any second.

Suddenly, Sebastian had an idea. The elevator bank on these floors was different than the express ones used by tourists for the observation decks. Maybe, just maybe, Sebastian could sneak onto one of these elevator cars and descent faster. He'd give anything not to have to struggle with all of those stairs below him. At the next door which read *61*, Sebastian listened carefully with his cupped, keen ears to see if there were any sounds on the other side. He could hear one person yell, "People need to stop leaving their lunches in this fridge for five years— this is absolutely disgusting!" Sebastian knew this floor was occupied, so he trotted down to door *60*. He listened carefully again and heard the whir of a copy machine moving in rhythm. Sebastian moved down to door *59* and this time when he listened, he heard silence. To be sure, he waited a few minutes and still heard nothing. He jumped up on the bar of the door to open it and it made a loud click that echoed in the stairwell. "Boy I hope there's no one on the other side," Sebastian thought. He pushed the door slowly and peeked through. The room was empty, only lit by a single emergency light on one wall and the overcast light through the windows. "This sure would be a great place to rest," thought Sebastian, "but I don't want to lose my chance to get into the museum today. Those men aren't going to waste any time on taking the Sub, so I have to be there as soon as I can."

Sebastian walked cautiously around the empty floor, still panting from his sprint down the stairs. It was dark. It was eerily quiet. But Sebastian soon spotted the elevator bank along the wall since the number panel above the door was lit. Sebastian could see the elevator was traveling up and down, from the lobby to the top floor, floor number 59. That was this floor. Sebastian thought, "Well that means the elevator car will arrive empty up here, but I forgot to consider the car could pick up people on the way back down." Sebastian was faced with a tough decision. He could either risk discovery on the elevator, but make it to the lobby effortlessly, or he could re-enter the stairwell and drain all of his remaining energy in the marathon decline. Sebastian was still panting from before and his stomach let out an enormous growl that echoed in the hollow room. "Ok, ok, you've put in your vote," thought Sebastian to his stomach. Sebastian decided to be brave and take a risk. He pressed the button with the down arrow, his paw slowly rising up to hit the button, now illuminated, and coming back to rest on the tile floor. When the elevator car grew near, a loud bell broke the dense silence. "DING!" Sebastian jumped, his body already flooded with adrenaline. But when the elevator doors parted, the car was empty. Sebastian stepped on and the doors closed behind him. There was no changing his mind now.

The car didn't move. It sat motionless. "What's going on?" thought Sebastian. "Why isn't this contraption working? I'm trapped in a cage like Clepticus!" Sebastian started to panic. But his outburst was immediately interrupted by Sebastian's realization that in his anxiety, he had forgotten to push a button! "Oh gosh, I'm so silly. I need to get my head on straight here," he thought. Sebastian hit the L button with his paw, but because his paw was so big, compared to the small and crowded buttons, the numbers 1 and 5 were also hit and lit up. Sebastian's eyes grew big when he saw the light display before him, knowing there was no way to cancel the selection, and nowhere to hide in the little box. The elevator descended and the digital numbers on the overhead panel ticked off the floors as Sebastian moved closer and closer to discovery. *55, 54, 53* . . . there was nothing he could do now. *50, 49, 48* . . . the car lowered itself into the shaft.

Sebastian thought, "If I can hide in this front corner and press myself close to the wall, maybe no one will see me from their office." The elevator seemed to take forever now, taunting Sebastian with either a dangerous fate or thin escape. *38, 37, 36* . . . "Oh geez, just hurry up so I can make my move and get on with this," thought Sebastian. His stomach rumbled in the safety of the elevator car, but was loud in the quiet nervousness. The elevator continued down at a steady pace. *25, 24, 23* . . .

"Come on! Come on! I'm ready for anything, let's go!" *20, 19, 18* . . . Sebastian was pacing in the tiny car, two strides one way, turn, two strides the other, never taking his eyes off of the number display.

12, 11, 10 . . . and he grew closer to his fate. Sebastian took his position, crammed against the front side of the elevator car, just under the number panel, next to a small glass door housing a red emergency phone. *7, 6,* and the car slowed to a stop. The doors parted open as a bell quickly and softly sounded, but loud enough to announce the car's arrival to those on the other side. Sebastian tightened his muscles to shrink into the corner of the car. He heard a woman talking on the phone, but nothing else as the doors paused, paused, paused, and then moved back together.

Sebastian was again concealed as the elevator gently, almost teasingly, moved again. Sebastian didn't even move from his corner, knowing floor one was on the way. The elevator stopped again as the number *1* was lit on the overhead display. The doors opened and Sebastian saw a foot and khaki pant-covered leg begin to step into the car. Sebastian felt his adrenaline surge and almost sprang from his corner through the door opening, but he saw the leg pull back and a man's voice declare, "Oh wait, it's going down, not up. That's weird." The doors closed.

Sebastian moved out of his corner and readied himself for the next floor, the lobby, which he knew would be busy and crowded. The elevator landed. "It's show time!" thought Sebastian. The doors opened and with instinct, Sebastian immediately surveyed his surroundings. He stepped out of the box slowly, as if ready for an attack, saving energy for a powerful escape, and he edged forward toward the light of the outside world. From around the back side of the elevator bank came a shrill scream. "Wolf! Wolf! Wild animal on the loose!" yelled a woman. Sebastian didn't even turn around to see who had spotted him and set off the alarm, so to speak. Instead, Sebastian took off as fast as he could through the droves of workers, still entering the lobby or grabbing a quick morning coffee. He suddenly saw his exit as the entire lobby froze, all action suspended in disbelief, interrupted by this unusual object of disorder. Even the uniformed man with a tower of muffin boxes, entering through the delivery door to the side of the now-motionless revolving doors stood still with the door open, frozen in awe at the instance of confusion.

Sebastian heard the sound of a security guard radioing his superiors. "We've got him back again. He's back down and in the lobby by the café. Send in animal control, quick, before this guy freaks out and goes nuts down here." Sebastian sprinted to the door, sheer speed, like a rocket on a windless, frictionless day. All was still and silent as Sebastian made a direct path to the open delivery door and slid through the escape before stunned brains could think to act. Sebastian was out of the Sears Tower. He was gone and already merged into the packs of workers on the sidewalk, moving with the flow like a fish in a school. Sebastian was at ease again, walking in a pack like at home with his buddies and Dominic. Sebastian moved with the crowd, south of the massive tower, along the sidewalks that took him away from danger to the museum. Sebastian had to arrive before the thieves so he could hide in the shadows and plan his attack. Not for a minute was Sebastian scared or overcome by the enormity of the mission before him. Never did he doubt he could do it. He was in charge. He would rely on his strengths.

Chapter 17: City of Big Shoulders

If Sebastian was going to have any physical strength to make it to the Museum of Science and Industry and then face the challenges of what would lie ahead, he knew he had to find something to eat. The rabbit meat shared by Clepticus had long since digested and turned into energy—and that energy had just been used up in the Sears Tower escape. As Sebastian paced with the crowd, he smelled something delicious, faint and sweet in the distance. He moved toward the smell. It was definitely meat of some kind. The crowd grew thinner and thinner. Soon Sebastian was walking alone in streets that were filled with construction equipment and empty lots, drawn along by the scent of the food. Iron I-beam structures rose from the ashes of old warehouses and cockroach-infested dwellings. Sebastian smelled the rats burrowed underground, nesting in communities like the ones above ground. He felt comfortable here since he looked like a stray dog, shaggy and running the streets.

He looked up at the street sign as the delicious meat smell grew stronger. The green street sign said Jefferson. Sebastian had no idea where he was, but he knew the smell was alluring and the museum was in this general direction—south. Sebastian trotted outside a brick building with large glass windows. Inside he saw a room full of tables and chairs, most of them filled with people and trays of food. Sebastian saw huge, tall sandwiches on their plates—heaps of pink corned beef sliced thin between two pieces of rye bread. "What is this heavenly place?" thought Sebastian. The sign above his head read *Manny's Deli*. Bowls of enormous matzo balls in soup, thick slices of meatloaf smothered in gravy next to potato pancakes, chop suey, slabs of salami on pumpernickel, and mountains of spaghetti, all was devoured by local aldermen and politicians, business men and women, firemen, police, even medical staff from nearby hospitals. Sebastian saw, and smelled, that this place was something special. He overheard two customers walking in the door. "This place has been around forever—heck, these guys first had their joint over on Maxwell Street. Too bad that's not there anymore, but lucky for us, we still have Manny's." The smell of corned beef drew Sebastian here, and now the legend kept him, hunting for a taste of that delectable dish.

Sebastian walked around to the back of the building where the back door was located. Two men in white pants and white buttoned coat-like shirts stood outside of the door, propped up against the cold brick wall, their arms folded in front of them to stave off the cold. They were visibly taking a break. Maybe they were even using the cold air to reenergize and grow more alert for the rest of their shift. The men chatted about the upcoming weekend and each looked around at the scene outside—construction cranes, trains, delivery trucks—when one of the men noticed Sebastian.

"Hey doggie!" he said loudly, but friendly enough that Sebastian knew they were not a threat. He stepped out from the shelter of the garbage dumpster so he was fully in view of the two men.

"Hey, he's a beauty—a big guy," said the one man to the other.

"You hungry big guy?" he asked Sebastian.

Sebastian sat down instantly and panted with his tongue hanging out, to communicate to the man that he was hungry and was ready for lunch. He couldn't bark in affirmation—after all, he wasn't a dog and didn't want to scare the men off by emitting a coyote howl.

"Alright guy, hang on here a second," said the man as he turned, opened the door, and went inside. The other man looked at Sebastian and smiled.

"Good thing you've got a warm fur coat on, doggie, because it is COLD out here! But you're probably used to these Chicago winters on the street, huh? I bet you're used to survival and a pretty smart guy. I bet you've been around the block a time or two, seen things you wished you didn't, and slept and ate where you had to, huh?" said the man.

Little did he know, Sebastian was just a tourist. Sebastian tried to play the role of a stray dog, looking up at the man with sad, upward eyes and a soulful smile. The back door opened and out came the kind man carrying a paper plate with a pile of corned beef scraps—the bits trimmed off of the customer's sandwiches with they ordered them "extra lean." Sebastian salivated as the dish was placed before him on the cold pavement. The heap of pink meat steamed and tantalized his nose.

"Dig in, boy!" said the man as he stepped away.

Sebastian told himself, "Okay, don't gulp it down. Even though you're really hungry, this is a special meal to be savored. This isn't the run-of-the-mill woods catch. This is cuisine." Sebastian put his nose to the steaming delicacy. He closed his eyes and inhaled the fragrant, even pungent, scent. It immediately made Sebastian salivate. The man's wrist watch started beeping before Sebastian could take his first bite.

"Alright Jim, that's the end of our break. Let's get inside and slave away," said the man. He turned to Sebastian. "You take your time and enjoy yourself now, and maybe we'll see you again sometime. You're always welcome here, big guy," he said, and they went inside.

Sebastian had privacy and fine fare. He was fueling up and had high spirits just before his momentous challenge. As he tasted and relished each scrumptious bite, juicy and full of flavor, he felt charged up, energy powering his body and mind. Sebastian loved corned beef on rye. Before long he had finished the entire portion and eaten a hole into the paper plate trying to lick and chew every last bit. Even as a coyote, he felt very full. Sebastian bowed his head in a moment of gratitude and appreciation in the direction of the door where the men once stood. He wished the men well and hiked along again to the Museum of Science and Industry.

Chapter 18: Express

Besides riding along Lake Shore Drive from Lincoln Park and seeing it in person, Sebastian had also once heard of Lake Shore Drive. Two people were riding their bicycles through the woods on a paved bike path near Sebastian's den last summer. It was a curvy street and the cyclists were going rather fast. One yelled to the other, "Hey, slow down! This isn't Lake Shore Drive, ya know!" So Sebastian recognized the name of the famous street, and its reputation as a quick thoroughfare through the city. He thought it might be a good route to take to the museum. Sebastian ran down the sidewalk on Roosevelt Street toward Lake Shore Drive. All of the people along Roosevelt were in cars, whizzing by, too engrossed in the traffic to notice Sebastian running by. When Sebastian reached Lake Shore Drive, he overheard two people talking across the street. The word *museum* in their conversation caught his attention.

"This is the Museum Campus over here, but it's only for the Field Museum, the Planetarium, and the Aquarium," said the woman.

The other woman replied, "Well can you tell me where the Museum of Science and Industry is located and how I can get there without driving?"

"You can go into the Museum Campus area and catch the number six, Jeffery Bus. It will express on Lake Shore Drive and take you to the Museum of Science and Industry. It's a ways from here in Hyde Park, so this bus is the best and quickest way to go," said the woman.

Sebastian wanted to save his energy for the big job of saving the Sub and didn't want to waste it on a long run to Hyde Park, so he decided he too would take this Jeffery Bus. Sebastian ran down the sidewalk and went underneath Lake Shore Drive through a beautiful tunnel with the words *Museum Campus* etched on the entrance above. When Sebastian got on the other side, he ran up a snow-dusted grass hill. It was crunchy and brittle under his paws. Sebastian thought, "Gosh, it sure is colder over here. I must be back by the Lake again. The wind over here is brutal." But Sebastian ran head first into the lake wind to a glass bus shelter he spotted at the back side of the Field Museum.

The bus shelter was empty except for one person who sat on the tiny wooden bench inside. Sebastian couldn't even tell if the person was a man or woman because the person was bundled from head to toe—hat, ear muffs, scarf around the face, sunglasses, long padded coat, heavy mittens, corduroy pants, and heavy bulky boots. The person sat huddled and didn't even notice the huge skeletal dinosaur to the side of them, let alone a little thing like Sebastian. Still, Sebastian stayed low and waited behind the bus shelter to be safe. It didn't take long for the bus to arrive and as soon as the door opened, Sebastian ran ahead of the bundled person and snuck in, undetected by the bus driver since she was looking at the boarding passenger. Sebastian saw that the bus was empty, so he decided not to be so bold as to take a window seat this time, as the driver would surely notice. Instead, Sebastian chose a seat in the middle of the bus and lay down underneath the seats.

The bus slowly inched out of the bus stop and Sebastian felt it make a few turns before picking up speed. The bus moved hastily down Lake Shore Drive and Sebastian wished he could see the sights, but his secrecy was more important. Even if Sebastian had been able to see out of the window, the scenery was only lake on one side and trees and shrubbery on the other. The exciting sights, sounds, and smells of the South Loop, Douglas Park, and Bronzeville were nestled behind the sticks of the winter trees. It was about a ten minute ride on the express bus and Sebastian was confident about his decision to ride rather than run. The bus slowed and Sebastian felt it turn a corner off of the Drive. The bus continued for about a block or so and then stopped. The front door opened and more passengers began boarding. Sebastian overheard the bus driver say to one of the passengers, "Hey there, Lou, how was security at the old museum last night? Any of the little chicks try to run away?" Sebastian realized this must be his stop, so he quickly bolted for the back door, pushed one of the slender panels with a thrust of his front paw, and went through the exit. No one even knew he had been there. Now, he thought, if he could just keep the same level of secrecy at the museum, he just might be able to pull off the big save.

Chapter 19: Secret Cargo

It was still before mid-day because the sun was not yet directly overhead, although it was getting very high in the sky. Sebastian knew he had to act quickly to find a position in the museum near the Sub where he could assess the surroundings to plan his attack. Sebastian saw lines of yellow busses unloading bounding school kids at the front of the building. The kids were hopping up the cement steps like little frogs, so excited about their field trip and experiencing life outside of the classroom. Seeing this only motivated Sebastian more. More than money could motivate thieves. Sebastian felt proud to have this challenge before him and he was confident he could pull it off. But Sebastian saw that this was not a good entrance to sneak into. Kids were a lot more perceptive and observant than adults, so surely they would notice a coyote among them.

Instead, Sebastian walked to the side of the building where large warehouse-like doors were open and men in dark blue pants and jackets moved huge wooden boxes with forklifts and trucks that beeped when they backed up. There was just enough distracting activity for Sebastian to slip inside undetected, he thought, so he approached the side of the building like a slinky fox—low to the ground and slow and cautious, always looking side to side with his eyes. No abrupt movements. There were only four men moving boxes, so Sebastian figured if he timed his entry, he could slip past all of them. He lay down in the crispy snow-dusted grass and just watched. Sebastian had to observe the way the men worked to see where and when he could run in. He noticed that the workers all moved toward the truck whenever a crate was unloaded. One man drove the forklift, another stood to the side of the truck door to guide the forklift driver, and two stood in the truck to move the crate onto the forklift.

Sebastian saw that he had a window of opportunity to move into the museum when the men were at the truck. He watched carefully as the forklift moved a wooden crate marked on the side with MSI in black letters into a freight elevator inside the museum's back entrance. After a few minutes, the forklift reemerged to load another crate. As the forklift neared the truck, Sebastian slithered to the limestone wall of the museum and peered over his long snout at the men. They were all engrossed in loading the crate so Sebastian moved swiftly into the back entrance of the museum, through the gigantic garage doors. He found himself in a room that housed wooden palates and large tools on the walls, like pulleys and ropes, with iron tracks along the ceiling. Sebastian ran along the side of the wall when he suddenly heard the *beep, beep, beep* of a second forklift backing up.

As the forklift neared Sebastian, the driver yelled, "Hey guys, how are things going in here? Need any help to speed things along?"

One of the men at the cargo truck yelled, "Watch out! You're going to back into that pile of palates along the wall!"

Sebastian stood frozen, hiding behind the palates, waiting to hear the sound of falling wood and feel the impact of the heavy pile on his body. He crouched down and squinted his eyes shut, tightening every muscle in his body as he heard the motor of the forklift stop.

"Who put these things here?" yelled the driver. As the men were yelling back and forth about who was at fault for the near collision, Sebastian, now full of adrenaline, sprung forward in a flash into the open back door. He was safely inside. At least, for the moment.

Chapter 20: The Craft of Being Covert

Sebastian stood in awe of the immensity of this glorious building. Inside he saw a tall ceiling that reached up to the sky. The room was enormous. So enormous that Sebastian saw an entire Boeing 727 airplane inside—its wing flaps moving and lights flashing. Sebastian had only seen these metal birds high above in the sky. He had no idea they were so large. "How could it really fly?" wondered Sebastian. He looked down another hallway in the huge room and saw a silver Pioneer Zephyr train. Sebastian had seen a lot of trains pass through the woods near his family den, but never one so shiny and beautiful. A conductor stood to the side and welcomed guests aboard. In the distance, Sebastian could hear the whistle of a coal mine as it echoed in the great hall, telling the coal miners it was time to begin work. Among all of the activity was a great cacophony of visitors, moving from hallway to hallway and exhibit to exhibit with either excited determination and focus, or wandering exhaustion.

Sebastian thought, "Boy, it's going to be tricky to keep out of sight here. This place is not like the Loop where everyone is in their own world. Here, everyone is watching everything and looking at their surroundings. Still, I must press on. There are hordes of people looking for the U-505 Sub and unless I stop this selfish plan, no one will be able to enjoy it." Witnessing the visitors' interest in the great vessel only fueled Sebastian.

He saw signs with a graphic of the submarine and arrows pointing in the direction of the exhibit. He saw that he had to cross the great room to the other side of the museum. The signs indicated that the Sub was at the front of the building. "I can't just run over there—everyone will see me," thought Sebastian. Just then, a museum employee began crossing the great hall with a wheeled cart full of food supplies and boxes piled on top and on the shelf underneath. The employee moved with his head cocked to the left side of his cargo so he could see where he was going. Sebastian immediately jumped to the right side of the cart and was shielded from the view of the visitors and went unnoticed by the museum employee. On Sebastian's open side was a massive toy train exhibition that kept people consumed with the moving engines and cars. Sebastian and the museum employee moved in tandem, like two tango dancers, across the glossy marble floor. They walked quickly to the other side and as the cart moved toward the elevator at the front of the building, Sebastian parted and dodged behind a large sign displaying the submarine's internal layout. There, nestled behind the great shield of a sign and a wall, Sebastian paused to catch his breath and collect his thoughts.

The spontaneity of his cross-museum passage had shaken Sebastian slightly, but he was contented to be just outside of the Sub exhibition and didn't want to risk getting caught now. He had come too far. "Maybe I should find a way in and just wait until the museum closes. Then I can move where I really need to be without being sighted," he thought. Even though Sebastian had obviously never seen the U-505 exhibit before, he felt that the best place to hide out while the museum closed would be inside the Sub itself. "There have to be plenty of nooks and crannies for the U-boat crew. I'll just stake out my little post and watch events develop in secrecy," thought Sebastian. He peeked into the exhibit and saw a hallway that displayed signage and photos of the Sub and its German crew. "Well, I can't get in that way, that's for sure," thought Sebastian. "I've got to find something better. I wonder what's behind these panels of text and photos," he thought. Sebastian could see there was a small amount of space between the exhibition panels and the actual plaster wall of the hallway. "Geez, how am I going to squeeze in there? I know my fur is fluffy and will scrunch down a bit, but I almost have to be a rat to squish into that tiny space," thought Sebastian. But he realized he didn't have much of an alternative. This was the only way in. Except for the exit, but who knew where that was.

He was here at the mouth of the Sub that once moved beneath the waves and now rested below ground, seemingly safe, but unaware of impending danger. Sebastian felt a connection to the Sub beyond this important call of duty. He felt akin to the Sub. He too had ridden the waves and would now descend below the ground to face impending danger. Sebastian felt the U-505 Sub was in some way his brother. And he hadn't even met the Sub yet. At least, not face to face.

Chapter 21: Behind the Wall

Sebastian was eager to meet the new member of his pack. He didn't waste any time and slid into the space behind the panel. "Mmmpf," said Sebastian with his mouth closed, but still, it was audible. "Had anyone heard?" he wondered, but nothing happened. So Sebastian continued through the tiny tunnel. "Oh my ribs!" thought Sebastian. "And what is holding these exhibition panels up?" Just then, Sebastian found himself confronted by a metal brace anchored from the panel to the wall. "Oh geez, I'm supposed to squeeze myself through here like a sardine and now I have to deal with an obstacle course? I want to save the Sub, not enlist for Sub duty—what is this, boot camp?" After he was done complaining to himself, Sebastian tried to crouch down as much as possible and still be able to propel his body forward. "Whoo-hoo!" cried Sebastian as his thigh muscle seized up in a cramp. But the thick panel of the exhibit muffled the cry from the crowd on the other side. "Walk it off, walk it off," Sebastian told himself, but there was nowhere to go. He straightened his back leg out and the pain subsided. "The faster I move, the faster I'm out of here—get going!" Sebastian said to himself. He crouched down again and scooted underneath the metal brace. He crawled like a sniper, pushing his entire body along the floor with his hind legs. When he was cleared of the brace, he rose up again and squeezed himself along. Now that he had mastered passing the first brace, passing each one was no more difficult and he could see the end of the panels up ahead.

Suddenly, Sebastian heard a voice coming from, strangely, above the panels. "The Battle of the Atlantic's high point came on June 4, 1944, when the German U-505 was seized by the USS Guadalcanal, led by Captain Daniel V. Gallery. It was the first time an enemy war vessel was captured in the ocean by U.S. sailors since 1815." At first, Sebastian thought the speaking man was a tour guide or museum employee. But when the narration repeated itself over and over, Sebastian realized it was just a recording, like the one he had heard in his elevator ride up the Sears Tower. Sebastian continued toward the end of the panels and heard another voice. "The Enigma machine, seen here, was captured on the U-505 and may have helped to shorten the war by a year or more. With this cipher machine, U.S. governmental code breakers were able to intercept and de-code messages sent by Nazi Germany. You will notice Enigma's elaborate system of rotors, a plug board, keyboard, and lamps. These parts worked in conjunction to encrypt and decrypt war strategy." Sebastian wished he could see the Enigma, but he continued slithering and scrunching along. He heard voices of sailors describing the capture and sound effects like metal doors closing and water. But the panels ended and Sebastian, still hidden in safety, looked out into the large room that held the beloved vessel. He decided he would lie down here and wait for the museum to close before he moved into the chamber, for it was too filled with voices and activity.

Chapter 22: Meeting Kin

Sebastian rested behind the Sub exhibit panel, where he was privately hidden from the masses of visitors on the other side. Ahead of him was the chamber that housed the Sub, which still remained out of his view. He could hear visitors commenting about the Sub's torpedo suspended from the ceiling in the chamber. He heard other voices saying, "Let's listen to the theatre presentation first," and, "Let's check out the tiny room where the German sailors slept." Sebastian couldn't wait to see the fantastic exhibit on his own. Sebastian could also clearly hear the audio from the theatre presentation. The narrator told the history of how the Sub was captured and how it made its way down the St. Lawrence River to the Great Lakes and finally to Chicago. The timbre of the narrator's soothing voice combined with Sebastian's exhaustion sent him into a deep slumber, his snout resting between his paws on the warm tile floor. Sebastian was warm, cozy, and safe. And now, he was sound asleep.

Sebastian dreamt he was back home in his family den with his mom, dad, and Dominic. He dreamt that a giant yellow forklift was headed toward his family den and was driven by two men dressed in black trench coats and fancy shoes. "There's the den," said the one man to the other, "Let's pick it up and carry it away forever," he said. The other man just laughed a sinister cackle and continued driving.

Sebastian was so frightened by the dream, and the sound of the insidious laugh, that he woke up with a jolt. He looked around, disoriented, and didn't see walls of dirt, or his family, as he expected. Instead he found that he was nestled between the museum wall and exhibit panel. But the lights were off and there was no sound of chattering people or the noise of clicking shoes on the tile. The museum was closed. Even though the room that housed the Sub was now dark, Sebastian was ready to venture out to see it. He was nocturnal and could see well in the dark, and he squeezed out of his tiny tunnel into the great Sub room. Sniffing for the smell of old steel and using his nighttime viewing abilities, Sebastian walked underneath a giant torpedo and suddenly came to the massive vessel.

"Oh!" thought Sebastian as a chill moved like a snake over his fur-covered body. "It's so big—how did it ever get here," he wondered in complete awe. "How did this thing ever float and swim?" Even though the structure was massive, Sebastian didn't feel small next to the Sub. He didn't even question for a minute how he would protect the treasured U-505 Submarine. He didn't wonder about his skill or ability and he didn't feel unable to perform the important task ahead. Instead, Sebastian thought to himself, "I must do it. I will do it. It is more special than I could have imagined. I am its keeper. I am its protector. I respect this vessel and will preserve it for all to enjoy." Sebastian made this vow to himself as he moved to an entrance to see the Sub from the inside. "Surely I can stake out a place in here where I can hide and wait for the thieves," thought Sebastian, as he entered the open door of the Sub.

Chapter 23: Member of the Crew

The cut-out entrance to the interior of the Sub was located in the back part of the craft. Sebastian walked through the large opening and found himself surrounded by light grey painted pipes and machinery. Thin pipes ran in straight lines along the ceiling, then serpented from red valve covers to pressure monitors and gauges. This was the Electric Motor Room. Valves and dials remained as they were almost 60 years ago and seemed eerily frozen in time. Thin metal grates allowed passage from this room to the next, along the length of the Sub. But Sebastian saw that the next room was similar in appearance to this one and there weren't any places to hide out. So Sebastian turned toward the back of the Sub and saw three metal stairs leading up to a hole in the wall. The round door to this room was open as well, so Sebastian climbed the stairs and stepped through the hole into the next room. "I must be in the Aft Crew and Torpedo Room," thought Sebastian. He had learned the terms "aft," for the back of a boat, and "fore," for the front of a boat, from Gio Botteghe, the young beaver back home, who frequently saw boats going up and down the rivers his family built upon. And the torpedo canisters lay in full view of Sebastian at the back of the tiny room. The canisters were round, white, and menacing. They were storage areas for destruction. Sebastian felt uneasy in their presence, but the bunks that hung from the wall made this location, despite the torpedoes, ideal for thief waiting.

The bunks were stacked one on top of the other and a few of them even folded up vertically to allow for more passage in the room. These bunks contained thin grimy-colored mattresses and a ratty pillow. "I know these beds are over 60 years old, but how could anyone get any sleep on these things?" questioned Sebastian. Still, he could see they were the ideal hideout. When the metal bed frame was up in its storage position, the bunk provided the perfect place to see when any movement occurred, and no one would be able to see Sebastian, especially since they would never expect a coyote in a crew bed. Sebastian climbed up the underside of the lower bunk, which was folded up, and was almost like a ladder to the second bed. "This isn't so hard to climb," thought Sebastian, as he dived head first into the top bunk. It was bumpy and hard, but Sebastian tried to nestled as snuggly as possible into the mattress, pillow, and scratchy wool blanket. He could clearly feel the hard mesh of the wire mattress support through his fur.

From the shelter of his crew bed, Sebastian could see two flashlights shining, aiming up and down the length of the Sub. Sebastian froze.

"I thought I heard something but everything is hunky dory over here, how about you?" said one security guard in his walkie talkie.

"Yep, good here too. That's the last check on this run— let's get back to that poker game so I can win some of that cash back from you," the other security guard replied.

Sebastian settled down again and imagined the Sub, surfacing to travel at fast speeds with a convoy; or gliding just below the surface with its undetectable periscope scanning the seas before launching a destructive, evil torpedo; or submerging deep below the waves to move slowly and covertly below the waves, moving deliberately to its next location. "I bet there were torpedoes hidden in these planks in the floor, right alongside the crew when they slept," thought Sebastian. "And I remember hearing one of the recorded voices in the exhibit hallway say that there were more crew members than there were beds, so I bet I'd have to either sleep during the daytime, to rotate shifts, or sleep alongside another crew member in this same bed," he imagined. "And all underneath me, there would be boxes and boxes of food, because they had to store it all somewhere. After all, the galley must be small and the voyages out to sea were long," thought Sebastian. "Hmmm. I remember seeing a small toilet over there, but no showers. I expect that the crew didn't smell too good after being down here for a few weeks, and my keen sense of smell can faintly detect the diesel fuel used to run this Sub's massive engines. I can only imagine the combination of human stench, diesel, and maybe a little brine from the salt water wafting through these passages. And another thing—there aren't any windows down here, as far as I can see, so I guess the crew would get pretty pale without any sunlight for such a long time. I'm not sure that life on this Sub was very easy. I'll stick with my family den," Sebastian thought.

He must have been visualizing life at sea for a while because he heard a knocking on the side of the Sub and he could tell it wasn't the security guards again. This knocking wasn't made by a flashlight searching for intruders. This was the sound of intruders searching for their prize, and they had just found it.

Chapter 24: Dismantle

"I have a seam over here," one of the men radioed to another. "I'm going to get started with this piece then before moving to the back—send over two others to help me here and you and the rest of the team take the front," he continued.

Sebastian now knew their plan and could prepare his defense.

"Let's move quickly, team," the man again radioed. "We only have until sun up to get this beast down the deep tunnel, and that's only six hours from now, so let's see some hustle out there," he concluded.

Sebastian was surprised at how fast the men had been assembled and how the dismantling process was immediately beginning. These thieves were smart, Sebastian realized. They had mastered stealing the U-505 and they had an intelligent plan to carry it out. What they couldn't have possibly prepared for, Sebastian thought, was him. No thief could imagine that a coyote lay in wait inside of the Sub, ready to foil the entire mission. When the time was right. Sebastian heard a humming constant noise and could see a red beam of light coming through the wall of the Sub down past the diesel engine room. They were using a laser to take the Sub apart. "I was wondering how they planned to get this humongous craft out of here," thought Sebastian. "It looks like they've got some high-tech methods and must have recruited some pretty high-tech guys." The sound made by the laser was so subtle that Sebastian knew no one in security could hear it.

"Okay team, we're through panel one and are ready to begin removal," said the man in his radio.

Sebastian peeked out from his bunk and saw the entire left side panel of the diesel engine room pull away from the Sub, leaving a gaping hole—a terrible wound in the vessel. He saw the men walking away with the panel. There were five of them on one side of the large metal panel and they carried it with ropes anchored on the top edge and round mechanisms that looked to be electro-magnets or vacuum suction devices of some sort. Sebastian wasn't exactly sure of their methods of removal, but he noticed that the men were all on one side of the massive metal panel. This meant that the panel would act as a shield on the other side, allowing Sebastian to travel with the thieves to the Deep Tunnel. And it was in the Deep Tunnel that Sebastian would deploy the idea he had for saving the Sub. This plan was foolproof and would destroy the evil operation.

Sebastian again heard the sound and saw the light of the laser. This time, the laser was in the Electric Motor Room, one room away from Sebastian. "I think now is the best time to make my move," thought Sebastian, "Because if anything goes wrong, at least I'll still have another chance." Sebastian silently sprung from his top bunk and landed with the agility of a cat, all four paws on the floor below. But his grace was of no use to the squeaky metal hinges holding the frame of the bunk to the wall. The immediate retraction of the 60 year old steel let out a loud "eeech!" that echoed through the hollow of the U-505. Sebastian froze and the laser shut off.

"What was that?" a man radioed.

"I'm not sure," the laser operator radioed back, "I'll have a quick look around."

Instinctively, Sebastian bolted into the tiny crew bathroom and jumped up onto the toilet. He held still, although the adrenaline running through his body made him want to breathe really hard and loud. He tried to inhale and exhale as silently as possible as he saw the beam of a flashlight shine down the length of the Sub. Footsteps were getting closer and Sebastian tried harder to suppress his panting. He was starting to feel faint from lack of oxygen. The flashlight beam scanned the Aft and Torpedo Room and rested on the bed frame.

"It's nothing," the man radioed to the others. "It was just a squeaky bed frame jarred by the movement of our work," he said. "Let's get back to what we're all doing right away. We don't want to lose any time," he finished.

The man retreated from the interior of the submarine and went back to his post lasering the wall of the Electric Motor Room. Sebastian, relieved, rested for a moment with all four paws still on top of the toilet and attempted to catch his breath from the adrenaline overflow.

"I'm through, send over the removal team again," radioed the laser man.

Sebastian silently stepped off of the toilet and exited the tiny bathroom. He crawled through the hole that served as a conduit between the Aft Crew and Torpedo Room, and the Electric Motor Room and snuggled close to the wall as it moved away from the vessel. Many of the gears and pipes and machinery that rested along the interior of the wall remained upright as the wall panel moved away. The motors and mechanisms were attached to the floor and were too heavy to budge. Sebastian had to rapidly maneuver around the contraptions to stay glued like a magnet against the shield of the wall. He moved exactly as the wall moved. He walked at the same pace. He paused when the wall paused. He was graceful. He was waltzing, turning in unison, mirroring every movement. He didn't know the path the wall took, but he knew where it was going—down the Deep Tunnel. And so was Sebastian.

Chapter 25: Getting In Place

The Sub wall went through a dark hallway and Sebastian observed that the men had lights somehow attached to their uniforms—perhaps on hard helmets. Still, Sebastian didn't need the light to see. His eyes were keenly adept to seeing in darkness and he could tell that he was in a hallway that was not used by the public. There were no exhibits and there was no signage. The men walked steadily and slowly down the corridor, careful not to create any unusual noise. And Sebastian was vigilant about his claws tapping on the tile. He intentionally tried to walk on the pads of his paws so he was clandestine behind the shield. He was covert. He was the secret weapon that would reveal the evil plan. And he was right there all along, undetectable below the exterior of the Sub, getting closer to the moment of attack.

The panel went onto some sort of a large wooden lift. The men turned the panel so that the side with Sebastian was leaning up against the wall of the lift. Sebastian was concealed in the space along the floor, and so he waited for the thieves to take their next step. He'd be right there with them. The door to the lift remained open and the men left. Suddenly, Sebastian could see another man arrive at the lift. He stepped onto the wooden plank and pulled a lever that brought two steel doors together. He then pushed a button and the lift jolted and jerkily descended. Sebastian could see that the man wore a security uniform, similar to the ones worn by the real security guards. He was an imposter. He was a thief. Sebastian felt the lift go lower and lower into a level many feet below the museum surface. The ride down continued for only a few minutes when the lift came to an abrupt halt. The imposter guard raised a lever and the two massive gun metal grey doors opened to another hallway. The imposter guard left the lift and radioed to the team down below on the subterranean level.

"Ok, panel two has arrived. Send in the removal team," he said as he walked away, down the dark hall.

Another team of five or six men arrived and stepped onto the lift. The served the same function as the team on the level above. They all stood on one side of the panel and attached ropes and their high-tech handles to the surface of the steel. They pulled the panel away from the wall where it had rested.

"Uhhh!" cried one of the men.

"Oh Jim, you big wimp," grunted another member of the team. "This thing might be a little tough because of its size and all, but you just wait until all of the engines and that massive propeller comes down," he said. "You better get ready for it too because this mission is going down fast, before sun up, and everything has got to be in that Deep Tunnel by then or else we're all out of luck and in the Big House again, you hear me? I'm NOT letting that happen. So suck it up and let's go!"

The panel exited the lift and Sebastian moved in unison. They took the panel only a short distance and propped it up next to the first panel. Both panels now rested along a cold limestone wall. Again, Sebastian hid in the nook created by the lean of the panel against the wall. And he waited. Shortly, Sebastian heard the lift ascending to the men above again. The lift motor paused and was silent. In fact, without the noise from the lift, there was no sound at all. Sebastian could hear his own breath moving in to nourish his body with oxygen, and then out to cleanse his lungs. He could hear the steady ringing of his blood flow, his entire head a humming circulatory symphony. Sebastian was in tune with his own body. The lift motor began running again, bringing down the next panel from the Electric Motor Room of the Sub. The men were dismantling the U-505 quicker than Sebastian anticipated would be possible. But the skill of the men, and the quantity used, in conjunction with a machine-like strategy, moved the theft of the Sub along at a lightning-fast pace.

"Alright," said a voice. "We're ready to begin the first load down to the Deep Tunnel now." Sebastian instinctively rose to attention.

"Three panels is the weight limit here and I've estimated to maximize efficiency that three is the perfect amount," he babbled with some nervousness.

"Okay, professor," one of the men carrying the panel responded sarcastically. "Just tell us where to put these things and you keep your research and calculations to yourself, okay? No hard feelings, or anything, I'm just bustin' your chops. You get us through this, professor and we'll have a good laugh about it later," he finished.

Chapter 26: Into the Depths

The professor spoke. "Let's move the three panels over here to this platform and attach these braces." He then radioed, "I'll need the Tunnel Team over here right away for this and to begin removing the entrance to the chasm."

Momentarily, the sound of boots sternly walking to the center of activity came thundering from out of the darkness. The panel team moved the first panel into place on the platform and attached the braces into place, while the tunnel team used a series of tools and hydraulic lifts to remove a heavy metal plank in the floor. The sound of the plank raising and sliding along the limestone reverberated along the walls and echoed throughout the underground passages.

"Alright," said the professor. "Let's hook up the pulley system just like we practiced at the loft," he said.

The men took a panel, moved it onto a cart of some kind, and immediately came for the next one where Sebastian was hiding. Sebastian moved as if he were glued to the plank. As it moved onto the cart, so did Sebastian. He was now nestled in a tiny space along the floor of a metal cart that was like a cage without a top. The last plank was loaded into place and the men began scurrying to assemble ropes and pulleys to some apparatus above that Sebastian couldn't see. Within minutes, the cart rose slowly off of the limestone ground. The cart swung slightly back and forth like a pendulum on a cable. The men steadied the cart and, along with the help of the apparatus, maneuvered the cart to the hole in the ground and positioned it to fit. The professor spoke to the men working the apparatus.

"Begin descent," he said with authority. "All hope abandon, ye who enter in!"

A quiet motor noise started nearby and the cart lowered through the floor. There was complete darkness. A small breeze wafted up through the shaft. Any voices that may have once been heard above were now completely silent as the cart continued down, and down, and down. Sebastian was not afraid of falling.

"I know these men have taken great care in planning and executing this heist, and certainly there is much less risk of discovery now than before in the elevator of the Sears Tower," thought Sebastian. So in a way, Sebastian felt practiced too.

The cart descended through the shaft at a steady pace, and Sebastian thought it had been lowering for a very long time. "I know the sign at the Sears Tower said this tunnel was 200-300 feet below the ground, so I guess it just takes a while," he thought. Soon, a dim light shining on the rough limestone walls illuminated the shaft. Sebastian could see the grey-white bumpy sides of the passage into the tunnel system. It reminded him of the nearby quarry back home. The amber light grew brighter and brighter and Sebastian felt that he was nearing the bottom and he would have to immediately scout out a hiding place where he could wait for the perfect time to unleash his strategy. Below, Sebastian could hear more men who likely comprised the tunnel team.

"Here it is guys," said one of the men in a normal volume, rather than the whispers and radio-talk upstairs. "Everyone get ready to unload this baby fast because it's just the start of the good things to come. Remember why we're all here—money. Now let's go!"

The foreman gave a sort of pep talk, like the captain of an army. Sebastian felt the cart hit the floor. "Bang!" It echoed loudly through the cavernous tunnel, and vibrated the bones in Sebastian's body. "That wasn't exactly a soft landing," thought Sebastian. "But still, it lets me know, my plan is going to work. This is going to be terrific!" the men disengaged the necessary parts of the apparatus, removing ropes and clamps, braces and supports.

"All five of you, let's get the first panel out of here," said the foreman.

Again, Sebastian heard the sound of scurrying boots clicking on the limestone ground. He heard the panel slide on the metal of the cart bottom.

"No! Not like that, you guys, you're going to mangle the seam on the bottom," and the men immediately stopped, now aware of their mistake. "We have got to get this baby back together in original shape or none of us will see a dime!" the foreman shouted with disdain. "Now let's not be so lazy this time and PICK IT UP!" he shouted.

"We got it, we got it, Augie," responded one of the men.

As requested, the men boarded the cart and lifted the panel with their ropes and suction handles repositioned now. The scuttling boots were louder now, and slower, heavy with the weight of the metal slab. Sebastian saw the men carry the panel over to a transportation system of some sort that had been constructed by the team prior to the execution. Sebastian couldn't see the entire system, only that it contained wheels and was extremely sturdy looking. It appeared to be made of parts from a coal transporter, from what Sebastian had heard his cousins from Southern Illinois describe.

When the men came to move panel two, behind which Sebastian was hiding, he readied himself to bolt in the other direction, so as not to be noticed. His muscles were taut and anticipating action. The second panel rose inches off of the cart and moved off. The men then positioned the panel near the first one as Sebastian darted into the darkness of the tunnel in the opposite direction. Because of his keen eyesight in the dark, Sebastian could tell the dark tunnel was empty on this side of the action, and he slipped into concealment.

Chapter 27: Vanished

Sebastian watched as the men removed the final panel off of the cart. The cart moved back up the shaft and the tunnel team secured the panels onto the coal transporter apparatus. Sebastian retreated even deeper into the black hole, waiting for the right time to explode and unleash his power. He watched the men. He saw them move like soldiers under the command of their foreman. They assembled the panels on the coal hauler, which contained multiple cars like a train. They did not send the transporter out and instead waited to load it with more cargo. The next shipment arrived from above. More panels were unloaded and moved to the transporter. The men sent the cart back up for another load of the stolen Sub parts.

As Sebastian waited patiently for the right time, he saw more and more of the sub come down into the Deep Tunnel— diesel engines; a propeller; batteries; torpedoes; air compressors; electric motors; a fresh water making machine; bunk beds; a rudder; steering mechanisms; radar units; doors; periscope tubes; the conning tower in multiple sections; a gun from the gun deck; a stove, refrigerator, and oven from the galley; hammocks; mattresses; flooring; and even a small crane and chain that was likely used for loading the torpedoes into the tubes.

Although the entire process of moving the U-505 Sub, piece by piece, had taken all night and all morning, Sebastian was in awe of the fact that they had pulled it off. The coal transporter had taken many of the parts down tunnel to another storage location and returned for more and more. The Sub was completely removed from the museum. It was gone. It had vanished, literally overnight. Sebastian was sure that the crew upstairs had dispersed since the museum would likely open soon, although he had no concept of time since he couldn't see the sun so far beneath the ground.

The crew that stood just a short distance from Sebastian now took a break, opening thermoses of hot coffee and eating something that smelled like whatever was in the delivery boxes at the Sears Tower—probably muffins or donuts or some other pastries. They gorged on the sweets and gulped their beverages like gluttonous kings. Soon Sebastian saw the cart from above descend one final time into the tunnel. Sebastian had figured wrong. The crew upstairs had not disappeared. They now entered the tunnel cavern via the cart. There were an additional dozen guys that loudly started boasting and cheering as they met up with the Deep Tunnel team. When they landed and disembarked, they all slapped each other on the backs and gave high-fives.

Witnessing such revelry made Sebastian feel angry. "How can they feel joy at taking away thousands of peoples' fascination and education?" Sebastian thought. "Can money really do this to people? Make them ignore so much? Make them not see the damage they cause? Make them hurt people and do things they know is wrong? Do they think that money makes it all okay? Does the money allow them to sleep soundly at night and carry themselves normally through the day? Do they feel unchanged after the act? Have they not been altered at all? Have they not lost even a little bit of their souls? Or are they just prepared and seasoned for the next time, ripened like a piece of fruit that falls from the tree to the ground?"

As baffling as these thieves were to Sebastian, he knew deep down that people were good—that these men were not representative of anything at all, except the criminal mind. "I know the whole reason why the Sub is here at the museum in the first place is to show people a piece of history and maybe even to warn visitors about man's destructive abilities. I know this Sub allows grandfathers to talk to their grandchildren about their experiences and pass on the history to future generations. Heck, it might even inspire future engineers, electricians, mechanics, inventors, sailors, leaders, or maybe a cook or two after seeing the galley! I know that people are more capable of good than evil and I'm going to finally put an end to this sinister scheme!"

Chapter 28: Unleashing the Beast

With all of his energy, summoned from all he had witnessed and all he had heard, for all of the people that had seen and would one day see the Sub, for his comrade that now lay in pieces below the city, Sebastian took a deep breath, filled his lungs to capacity with the stale air of the massive tunnel and thought, "I am going to do this! Help me Clepticus!" as he released it all into a deep, thundering, "WHOO, WHOO, WHOODOOOOOO!" It was the pack howl. And he repeated his howl again and again so that the commotion reverberated off of the bedrock, over and over. The cacophony was starling. All of the men immediately froze into a fearful stance, their eyes alert and looking without noticeably moving.

"What's that?!" whispered one of the men.

"I think it's the ghosts of the Sub crew!" yelled another man in a confused, panicked voice.

"NO!" hollered another man. "I know that sound from when I was a kid in Wisconsin! That's a pack of wild coyotes! Run for your lives!"

All of the men dropped their donuts and climbed onto the cart, shoving each other to get on board, jamming the cart full, and pushing one another.

"Move!"

"Hurry!"

"Get back!"

"Get off of me!" shrieked the frantic men on the cart that ascended into the air and entered the hole to the world above. What was a moment ago a celebratory band of criminals turned into a writhing mass of feet and arms entering the circle in the ceiling above. The yelling and confusion grew further and further away from Sebastian as the men disappeared through the tube.

Sebastian, safe from capture now, moved out of the shadows and into the light. The Sub was in pieces, but was still contained within the tunnel passage on the coal transporter flats. Sebastian walked over to the dissected vessel. "You're protected now," he thought as his eyes scanned the wounded leviathan. "You'll be put back together in no time." Still, Sebastian couldn't help but feel pity for the dismembered Sub. The U-505, once a center attraction for visitors all over the world, and a trophy won by the efforts of the men who captured her, now lay in pieces far, far underground.

And that is when it hit Sebastian. He was far, far underground too. He was three hundred feet below civilization. "How am I going to get out? How is anyone going to know I'm down here, or that the Sub is down here? How will we be rescued?" wondered Sebastian with dread. He was trapped. He was no different than Clepticus, howling in the zoo for laughs. Except Clepticus had food, water, and people who came to visit. Sebastian was hungry and alone. Despite having the Sub at his side, Sebastian was lonely, scared, and now that his thoughts were again his own, he missed his home. But would he ever see it, or the light of day, again?

Chapter 29: Chicago's Finest

Before Sebastian could experience his fear and anxiety for more than a moment, he heard the cage from above clang on the bedrock ground behind him. Startled, he let a "whoo hooo!" escape from his throat. He turned around to see two men in police uniforms shining flashlight beams in the direction of the wild sound. The beams hit Sebastian in the eyes and he lowered his snout to deflect the blinding light.

"Well, they weren't kidding when they said there were coyotes down here, but I think there might only be one—I don't see any more than that," said the one policeman.

"Well it is an echo chamber down here and if that guy got really howling at those thieves, and from the looks and sounds of things, he did, then I bet it does sound like a lot more than just one coyote down here," replied the policewoman.

Sebastian could tell these were good, smart people.

"And lookee what's behind him," said the policeman. "That coyote, believe it or not, is protecting the Sub!"

"He saved the U-Boat! He's guarding it and he scared off the thieves! This is amazing!" said the policewoman. "Hey, boy, come here! We'll take you up top where you can see the thieves being handcuffed and arrested. We'd like you to see it and we'd like them to see you too!" she said.

Sebastian didn't hesitate to approach the police. "They get it," he thought to himself. "They can tell what happened here and I'm getting rescued!"

Sebastian climbed into the metal cage next to the two police who didn't show any fear that they were standing next to a wild coyote. Although, Sebastian wasn't so wild anymore. He had seen too much of city life to be wild. He had witnessed the evil that men were capable of, like stealing a Sub or even creating a Sub in the first place. And he had witnessed the good that humans could show too, feeding him terrific food when he needed it most. Sebastian now was riding back up to the city with good people who saved his life and were feeling appreciation for him. He knew that Chicagoans were good people and Clepticus was right. This was a good city and Sebastian looked forward to seeing it again.

"Hey big guy, I bet you're hungry too, after your adventure," said the policeman. "We'll make sure you get some good grub up top. Maybe some good pork chops or ribs from Carson's. Let's get him that," he said.

"Yeah, we'll make sure to put a plastic bib on him—and order enough for the police force and security guys here. We'll all have a little feast for lunch," the policewoman said.

"And we'll get some slaw and those au gratin taters too," the policeman finished.

The cage reached the top and another man in a police uniform held the rope that was woven through a multi-pulley system. He wrapped the rope around a pole and secured it with a fancy knot as Sebastian and the two other police disembarked the contraption.

The policeman spoke. "Well guys, you're never going to believe this." Sebastian and the two police were standing in front of a group of law enforcement and security personnel. "This guy right here," and he pointed to Sebastian, "This guy here is responsible for saving the U-Boat!"

The group of men looked surprised and hung on the next word.

"The Sub is dismantled, but every piece of it is down there in that Deep Tunnel."

There was an audible breath of relief from the group.

"This coyote howled and howled, and that's how all of the thieves came running out of the tunnel like a bunch of rats," he said. "We owe a lot to this guy here—heck, Chicago owes a lot to him. I say we all go upstairs and give the sergeant at the station a call and then put another call into the mayor's office and let him know that he's got a true Chicagoan here—a real hero," he said, as he gave Sebastian a firm couple of pats on his side.

Everyone boarded the lift to the top floor of the museum, and every hand on that elevator patted Sebastian out of respect and appreciation. "You're one of us now, big guy," Sebastian heard a voice in the group say. "You're one of the finest." When the elevator stopped, and the metal lever was lifted, and the two steel doors parted, there in the hallway on the other side were the thieves in handcuffs. They were held by more police and surrounded by even more. "Okay, guys, let's take them outta here," a policeman said. They all walked past Sebastian as they went toward the police cars waiting outside.

One of the thieves spoke as he approached Sebastian. "That thing there made all that noise? We were afraid of that? That mutt cost us $50 million dollars?"

Sebastian let out a "whoo hooo whoodoooo," right at the thief, to let him know he was not a mutt, and to harass him a bit.

The thief jumped and yelled "ahh!"

All of the police laughed and laughed. "Good one, big guy!" they said to Sebastian.

The thieves all left and rode away to be prosecuted. And before long, more cars arrived at the front of the museum by the front entrance. These cars contained bags and bags of Carson's ribs and chops and pepper steak and side dishes. The police crew and Sebastian celebrated, devouring the delicious meat, all hot and saucy.

One of the police turned to the crew and said, "You know, there's just one thing I don't get about this whole thing. How the heck did that coyote end up in the Deep Tunnel?"

"Hmmm" and "Yea" came replies from the group.

Sebastian just smiled a barbecue grin and thought to himself, "You wouldn't believe it all, even if I told you!"

Chapter 30: Media Hound

Sebastian spent the night on a toasty blanket at the police station on 35th Street and Michigan Avenue. Sergeant O'Donnell, as he introduced himself to Sebastian the night before, made Sebastian a little makeshift bed out of newspapers and a red plaid wool blanket. After spending the day at the kennel with the other canine crew, Sebastian was pleased with the Sergeant's special treatment and fell sound asleep. And when Sergeant O'Donnell returned the next morning, Sebastian was still sleeping.

"Hey big buy, you just take your time waking up," said Sergeant O'Donnell. "I'm just going to do a little paperwork, but when you wake up, I have a surprise for you," he whispered.

Sebastian continued to laze around in the warm office, the morning sunlight streaming in through the window and onto his snout. He normally wouldn't sleep this long, not on this kind of schedule, but that's what the city can do to you. Finally, Sebastian rolled over onto his back and stretched all four limbs in opposite directions. He wiggled back over and stood up. He looked up at the Sergeant and sat down on his hind quarters. The sergeant was watching him.

"Hey, big guy, I want to show you something." The Sergeant picked up a copy of the *Chicago Tribune* from the top of his metal desk. He read the headline to Sebastian and showed the paper to him.

"Wily Coyote Saves Sub," said the Sergeant. "You're famous, big guy! Everyone in the city knows what you did and are grateful to you for your hard work and courage. Not every coyote would've done what you did. Heck, not every human being would've done what you did. You're something special, big guy," said the Sergeant.

Sebastian felt terrific. What a great way to wake up!

"So, the city would like to thank you for all you've done. You're a hero to us, and the mayor has declared today Coyote Day. And the police force has a little something planned too. So, get ready to take a ride in a police cruiser down to City Hall!" the Sergeant finished.

Sebastian couldn't believe this reception for his work. "This really is the City of Big Shoulders," thought Sebastian. There really wasn't much getting ready for Sebastian to do. He stood up and looked at the Sergeant to let him know the day could begin. The sergeant pushed his grey steel chair back and stood up.

He grabbed the newspaper and a little box and said, "Alright big guy, let's hit it!"

Sebastian followed the Sergeant out of the small office into a large room that was circuitous with mazes of cubicles lit by large, buzzing florescent lights. He heard people behind the little walls whispering and saw them peeking out and then the entire room exploded in applause. The workers came out of their labyrinths, over to where Sebastian walked with the Sergeant, and stood, clapping their hands excitedly, smiling and staring at Sebastian. He stopped, looked at everybody, and let out a small, peaceful, "whoo dooo!" to say think you, and maybe even to give his adoring fans a little taste of what happened down in the tunnel.

The employees cheered even louder and Sebastian heard a few of them say things like, "Thanks Coyote!" and "You're a hero!" and even a "Welcome to the force!"

The Sergeant said to Sebastian, "Alright big celebrity, let's get movin'. The mayor is waiting for you!"

Sebastian followed the Sergeant out of the police headquarters as everyone applauded along the way. The Sergeant's police cruiser was parked along the front of the station in a designated spot.

The Sergeant opened the side door. "You can sit next to me, big guy. The back is for criminals, like the guys you met in the Deep Tunnel, so you sit up here," he said.

Sebastian climbed inside and sat on the vinyl seat. The Sergeant walked around and got in, started up the car to warm it up, and turned to Sebastian.

"Well big guy we have to buckle up—it's the law," and he reached over Sebastian for his seat belt and strapped Sebastian in to the seat. Sebastian felt a natural instinct to get out of this situation. He felt trapped. But he suppressed his instinct because he did feel safe with the kind Sergeant, and anyway, he was in the city and a whole new set of rules applied here. Feeling comfortable in small spaces just went with the city territory. The Sergeant put his own seatbelt on as well and backed out of his privileged parking place. The Sergeant drove out of the police station and turned onto the street.

"We'll take Michigan Avenue there so that you can see some of the sites out of the window," said the Sergeant.

Sebastian watched as the car passed new real estate developments, like South Commons, and new town homes. He saw beautiful, sleek architecture out of the sergeant's window. A sign said IIT.

"That over there is a sheath that covers the El train so there isn't as much noise for the college students. It was designed by Rem Koolhaas and the rest of the buildings there are the creation of Mies van der Rohe," said the Sergeant. "Architecture is very important to Chicago, big guy, and I must admit, I'm a bit of a culture buff myself," he said.

Sebastian witnessed construction cranes behind construction platforms along the street. The cranes were building skyscrapers, rehabbing old warehouses into expensive lofts, and new restaurants and shops. There were blues clubs and newspaper bureaus and busses and cars buzzing up and down the street. More high rises appeared when the police car got to the museum campus area on Roosevelt. Sebastian recognized this place. He caught the bus to the Museum of Science and Industry not far from here. The cruiser moved along Grant Park on one side, and older buildings like the Blackstone Hotel on the other. Then Sebastian saw the two lions he remembered from his trip to the Loop on the bus. The lions were green and flanked a large limestone staircase where people sat in small groups or trekked up to enter a building.

"That's the Art Institute of Chicago. Inside are great works of art by masters like Van Gogh, Manet, Moet, Renoir, Degas, Cezanne, and Seurat," said the Sergeant. "I could go on and on. Like I said, I'm a bit of a culture buff!" he finished.

The police cruiser turned off of Michigan Avenue and turned down a few other streets and arrived at a large limestone building surrounded by Greek columns around its midsection. The cruiser came to a final stop in a parking garage nearby and Sebastian and the Sergeant got out and walked to the City Hall entrance on LaSalle Street. They found a bank of elevators almost immediately inside the entrance and boarded one bound for the fifth floor. When they got to the mayor's office and opened the door, the administrative assistant was inside, looking at Sebastian with a smile.

"We've been waiting for you, Mr. Coyote," she said to Sebastian. The lady ushered Sebastian and the Sergeant quickly inside. She knocked on a large, thick wooden door and opened it slightly.

"Mr. Mayor, they're here," she said inside.

"Let them in!" Sebastian heard a loud voice respond.

The lady opened the door wide and gestured for them to go inside. The mayor stood up from behind a beautiful, massive desk on the other side of the room. Behind him were windows overlooking a fountain below and the exteriors of more buildings. Sebastian could look right inside the other offices and see people working at computers.

"Well," spoke the mayor, "I understand that the City of Chicago owes you a big thank you!"

Sebastian sat down on his hind quarters to show he was listening and that he was respectful of the mayor.

The Sergeant spoke, "Yes, mister mayor, we do. This guy saved the U-Boat, and it appears as though he went to great lengths to do so. With our canine team, we have tracked this coyote's scent from the Museum, onto Lake Shore Drive, strangely enough to Manny's Deli—"

"Oh," interrupted the mayor, "terrific choice—you've got good taste!"

"Then he was at the Sears Tower Observation deck, where the canines also picked up the scent of our two head thieves—the ones we picked up and arrested this morning. They've given us the information on the mastermind behind the whole scheme as well, so we have five patrols headed over to his property as we speak," said the Sergeant."

"Wonderful!" replied the mayor. "But where did this guy come from? That's what I'd like to know."

"Well, Sir, it seems we came across an animal control report from two nights ago that shows a control team was dispatched to Navy Pier after calls from neighbors came in saying that howling was heard coming from the breakwater. Apparently, the control team was unable to catch the coyote who fled further out along the breakwater. Sir, I suspect this is that coyote and that he arrived here on an ice drift," finished the Sergeant.

"Well, brave one," said the mayor to Sebastian, "you really are something. You've done a lot for us. And now, we'd like to repay you a little bit. Sergeant, and um, let's name you Chi-Town Coyote, please follow me," said the mayor as he walked toward his office doors.

The three walked down the hall to a room that held people assembled in every available chair. Most of them had small tape recorders or notepads and pens. There were large television cameras on tall tripods along one wall of the room. In the front, there was a small platform with a podium containing numerous microphones. On the wall behind the podium was the round seal of The City of Chicago. The mayor walked up to the podium. The sergeant and Sebastian stood next to him.

The mayor spoke. "Ladies and gentlemen of the press, we have a hero to honor today." The mayor told the story of how Sebastian came to discover the plot to steal the Sub and how he saved it from the thieves. "So today, we honor Chi-Town Coyote and mark this day officially Coyote Day to celebrate our hero and express our gratitude," said the mayor. The Sergeant stepped over to the podium and the mayor moved aside.

The Sergeant spoke and looked at Sebastian. "On behalf of the members of the City of Chicago Police Department, we would like to present you with this badge indicating that you are an honorary member of the Chicago Police Department."

He clipped a silver-colored badge onto the fur on Sebastian's chest.

"Can we have a few words from Chi-Town Coyote, for the record?" yelled a woman reporter. The Sergeant stepped aside and moved a chair to the podium. Sebastian hopped up on the chair and gave a quiet "whoo hooo whooodooooo!!" into the microphones as the press cheered.

Chapter 31: Metamorphosis

Sebastian began his walk back home along the lakeshore right after his time with the mayor and the Sergeant. It was hard to go, but Sebastian knew it was time to return home. Knowing his family could never possibly believe his exploits, Sebastian was sure to carry a copy of the *Chicago Tribune* containing his headline. The Sergeant had been kind enough to strap the newspaper to Sebastian's back with a piece of twine. Sebastian had walked for the rest of the day and all through the night and was now resting comfortably in his family den. Sebastian had plopped himself on the den floor and rested his snout between his outstretched arms, one paw on each side. Sebastian's mother sat next to him talking.

"I still can't get over it, Sebastian," she said.

"Well," replied Sebastian, "I did enjoy my time in the big city, and am happy I was able to help, but I must tell you, there's nothing like being at home. The smell of the creek and the birch trees and having my family and friends back, well, I missed all of this a lot."

Sebastian's father and brother Dominic walked into the room.

"We couldn't have imagined this is where you ended up," spoke Sebastian's father, looking at the newspaper.

The photo on the paper's cover told the whole story. Sebastian was pictured in front of the U-Boat and a crew of police bending down around him, smiling.

"Gosh, Sebastian," said Dominic, "You're a real hero, huh? My own brother, a hero! Wait until I tell the guys!"

"Well, it is a big deal," said Sebastian's mother. "You know I was worried about you when you didn't come home, especially after how upset you were about that chipmunk," she said.

"Oh my gosh. The chipmunk! I totally forgot about that little thing!" said Sebastian, as if he were a completely different coyote back then, only three days ago.

"Yeah, well I sent out red-tailed hawks to search for you, and when they came back with no sightings of you, I knew there was trouble," she said. "Little did I know you were floating to Chicago on Lake Michigan! I think it's a good thing I didn't know what was going on until afterward when you were here, safe and sound. As a mother, this is awfully hard, but I am awfully proud too," she finished.

Sebastian's father stepped forward. "Me too, Sebastian. Say, I know you're exhausted and everything, but what'dya say we take a little stroll outside and chat, you know, coyote to coyote?" he said.

"Sure dad," said Sebastian. "Let me just peel myself off of this floor!" Sebastian and his father walked outside of the den and stepped through the snowy woods.

"Sebastian," said his father, "remember when we talked before you left, or, em, drifted away? About being yourself, even if you're afraid?"

"Sure, dad, I remember," said Sebastian.

"Well I know you must have been afraid a lot of times over the past few days. I mean, I know that I feel fear just hearing about it," said Sebastian's father. "Well, I just want you to know that I'm proudest of you, not because of the U-Boat or the mayor or Coyote Day, or the police department, even though I am real proud of all of that. But I'm most proud of you because you were yourself. You were driven by your adventurous side and had to tap into your determination and your confidence, and even your anger and your instinct. I'm so happy to know you, Sebastian. I've learned a lot from my own son today," he said and he patted Sebastian on the back.

"Geez, dad, thanks. This is the greatest honor of all," said Sebastian.

"Now," said his father, "enough of that mushy stuff. Why don't you give me an example of that howl you used? Show me what you learned from your old dad!"

Sebastian let it rip. "Whoo hooo whoodooooo! Whoo hooo whoodooooo!" he howled.

"That's amazing!" said his father, who joined in the song. "Whoo hoo whoodoooo!"

About the Author

Heather Augustyn is a part-time newspaper reporter and magazine writer and a full-time mother of two little boys, Sid and Frank. She received her B.A. degrees in English and philosophy from Bradley University and her M.A. in writing from DePaul University. She lived in Chicago for ten years and now makes her home with her husband and sons in Chesterton, Indiana. This is her first book.

The illustrations in this book are linoleum cut block prints, printed by hand. They were created by the author.